The Dead Don't Bleed

ALSO BY NEIL ROLLINSON

POETRY

A Spillage of Mercury

Spanish Fly

Demolition

Talking Dead

The Dead Don't Bleed

NEIL ROLLINSON

JONATHAN CAPE
LONDON

3 5 7 9 10 8 6 4

Jonathan Cape, an imprint of Vintage, is part of the
Penguin Random House group of companies

Vintage, Penguin Random House UK,
One Embassy Gardens, 8 Viaduct Gardens, London SW11 7BW

penguin.co.uk/vintage
global.penguinrandomhouse.com

Penguin
Random House
UK

First published by Jonathan Cape in 2026

Copyright © Neil Rollinson 2026

The moral right of the author has been asserted

Typeset in 11.8/16.2pt Calluna by Six Red Marbles UK, Thetford, Norfolk
Printed and bound in Great Britain by Clays Ltd, Elcograf S.p.A.

The authorised representative in the EEA is Penguin Random House Ireland,
Morrison Chambers, 32 Nassau Street, Dublin D02 YH68

A CIP catalogue record for this book is available from the British Library

ISBN 9781787335363

For Helen

In Spain, the dead are more alive than anywhere else on Earth: their profile wounds like the edge of a barber's razor

—Federico García Lorca, *Theory and Function of the Duende*

córdoba 2003

The cemetery is just as Frank remembers it. He'll never get used to these Spanish graves, the niches, one on top of the other, like filing cabinets, hewn out of stone. The walls are thirty feet high in places. Step ladders stand at intervals, awaiting relatives, enabling them to reach the highest niches, to clean the dirt and dust off the marble fascias. To place their plastic flowers, their photographs, just inches away from the heads of their dead. How the soul must yearn for solid clay, thinks Frank, of being buried in the tribal earth. Not this scruffy-looking tenement of the dead and rotting, piled high.

You can smell the rot on a day like this. He takes off his hat and wafts it about his face. It's so hot he might be walking in a foundry. He wanders along the avenues, under cypress trees, oranges, lemons. Up close, the enclosures are like ovens: bread ovens. A few are empty and you can see the brickwork inside, held together by a rough, grey mortar. For the poor, instead of marble, their niches have been sealed with a skim of cement where the names of the dead have been scratched in with a twig, or a lollypop stick. The pathway is dusty and a fine powder rises at every footstep, coating Frank's black shoes. Nobody else is out. He looks up at the sky. Nothing. Just white. Like the heart of a furnace.

He thinks of his father in his cold, windswept grave-yard in Scotland. The sound of the angry sea, the ceaseless mewling of gulls. Rooks in the stunted trees. It would be raining there right now. He'd bet on it. What a blessing, to turn towards the sky and feel the cold sea spray on your face.

When he comes to her niche he stops and takes off his shades. She's on the top row, high above. He wheels the ladder along the path, settles it in front of the column and starts to climb. He feels dizzy halfway up, from the effort and heat. He grips the handrail. To think of her in there, desic-cated over the long, hot summers. He wipes the sweat from his face, but it gathers in his eyebrows, drips into his eyes. His shirt is drenched. When he gets to the top, he sees the legend is still clear: 'Lucía Moreno 1956 – 1989'. Her maiden name. His own name unrecorded, long forgotten. He'd missed the funeral. He hadn't been welcome. He doesn't blame them. If not for him, she'd still be here. God, how he misses her. It still hurts, all these years later. Around him, from every alcove the eyes of a hundred ceramic Christs watch him, a host of cracked and faded angels. They adore their trinkets, their plastic votives; the mass of kitsch that litters these places. You could climb to heaven on the stuff. Someone has placed, in a gilt frame, a photograph, which has faded almost to nothing.

Standing on the top step he looks beyond the cemen-terio. He can see La Mezquita, resplendent in the centre of

Córdoba, its bell tower pointing skywards towards some dumb, indifferent god. A cathedral built in the middle of a mosque. It still makes him laugh. This town is the embodiment of Spain, it seems to him. Harsh and elegant, cruel and comical. Ancient beyond imagining. The Moors loved it here. No wonder. Open fields stretch far to the south. The Guadalquivir, vast and powerful, pounds its way towards the Gulf of Cádiz.

This was their Spain. His and Lucía's. He remembers the summers they spent here, the golden triangle between Seville, Córdoba and Granada. Spain was still exotic and strange, and powerful then, as only a new place can be. He'd been dizzy with it all: the shadow and light, the scent of orange blossom, the endless, undulating fields and the high, unblemished sky. Her spirit too, passionate and indefatigable. La Petenera, he used to call her, after the beautiful, heartbreaking figure of southern flamenco. A palo so tragic it is said that even the great flamencos would refuse to perform it, or even listen to it, for fear of the ill fortune it might bring. She and the land had been indivisible. He couldn't imagine one without the other. How long ago it all seems now. Every time he returns it is a pilgrimage. Driving through the endless fields earlier, he'd thought of Lorca's horseman riding towards Córdoba, his pocketful of olives: *Córdoba, distant and solitary. Even though I know the roads, I will never reach it . . . death is watching me from the towers of Córdoba.* He turns and looks to the north; the vast central plains rise out of shadow. Madrid, he thinks, a few hours north and he wishes he was there.

To be among the smart, fashionable bars and restaurants of Sol and Malasaña. He's driving south however, to find his brother. To tell him their father is dead. That their empire of violence is finally over.

He climbs back down, stubs out his fag and kills it under his boot sole. Of all the lands of Europe this is the one where death is most at home, slouching through narrow streets, haunting the churches, taking coffee in the square. Always there. It's in the flag: the blood red and the searing solar yellow. The bullfights, the atrocities of the civil war. A country full of contradictions. It's why he loves the place. It has brought him more bliss and misery than anywhere could hope to promise.

He has a drink at a roadside cafe, at a table shaded by a parasol. It is quiet, peaceful. The waiter sees his book on the table: *Collected Poems of Lorca*. He picks it up and turns it over, then smiles at Frank.

'They kill my grandfather,' he says, his voice deep, gravelled, like a man who enjoys his cigarillos. 'Like Lorca,' he continues, 'his body is never find.'

'Lo siento,' says Frank.

The waiter shrugs and wanders off. When Frank calls for the bill a little later, the man waves it away with a lazy gesture.

'Cortesía de la casa,' he says.

Everyone has suffered. Frank leaves a large tip and gets up, into the savage heat. It seems to set his hair alight. He drives south. Next stop Cádiz and the Mediterranean. He feels a rising dread at the thought of seeing Gordon again.

He feels no animus towards him, though he can't speak for his brother. He remembers still, the anger, how the red mist would fall out of nowhere, the unfathomable rage and the flurry of balled fists, or worse, if there were implements close to hand. But much has changed in twenty-five years. He's changed. The world has changed. God knows what he'll find after all this time.

He travels across endless fields, vineyards mainly; sherry country, wheat already ripe and being taken in. The harvest is earlier here than at home. The land stretches forever. Nobody comes. They stick to the Costas. The roads are deserted.

He passes an abandoned church and pulls over. He walks back to look at the place. It's just a wreck: stones and rubble. The roof is gone, the window glass long since shattered. The walls, or what is left of them are fire damaged, cracked and blackened with smoke. The ruin stands in a barren land of stunted olives and almond trees. Nut casings crack in the vice-like heat. This land is beaten out of pig iron, brutal and unforgiving. Frank stands for a moment, taking it in. Republican country. No place for a priest or a nun. The sun blazes down, chromic, unrelenting. He walks into what is left of the nave and stands in the transept, at the dead centre of the cross. People sat here and sang and were happy, and then their families were butchered in the street. There's a condom, some beer cans and the charcoal of a small fire where local kids have been having some fun. There must have been a village here once. Torched in the civil war. Frank spits

5

on the floor. The church sided with Franco and this was the consequence. He has no sympathy; you'd think they would know where good resides. But they went with the king, with the forces of conservatism, fascism. Churches were burned, priests assassinated. Franco would have his day though. That's why there's nothing left here. It didn't end well for the Republicans.

He sits on a rock and drinks from a bottle of agua. What a place. There's no escaping its harsh geology. The yellow rocks burn, the air sizzles and the empty campo simmers in a heat haze. He takes photographs. He'll finish his book soon, then look for a publisher. He just needs a bit more research. *The Death of the Poet,* he'll call it. Perfunctory but precise. This is how it will start. And end. At the side of a lonely road, a gunshot in the middle of the night, then nothing.

ashington - northumberland 1978

They heave the sack from the boot of their Vauxhall Victor, one of them at either end, and sling it on the grass. Carol stands beside the passenger door smoking a cigarette, laughing as they struggle with the weight.

'You should bloody try lifting it,' says Frank.

He grabs their shovels from the boot as Gordon stretches his back and lights up a No 6. He seems bored already. Frank looks at his brother and wonders if he's going to be a help or a hindrance. He scans the surroundings: scrawny cottages and bungalows, a row of static caravans. A horse hangs its head in a field, as if in shame. There's a mattress sprawled under bushes, its guts hanging out. He can smell the sea. What a dump. They'd left Newcastle at two in the afternoon and driven up the A1 into Northumberland, under low skies. Almost Christmas, though you'd never know it, working their arses off day and night while the lads are down the pub, or the working men's club. Laurence has been easing them into the day to day, especially Frank: pickups, errands, deliveries. And now this: a big responsibility; testing Frank's mettle. *A man's job,* their father had said. *And take that pillock with you, see if you can knock some sense into him,* though Gordon, as ever, is in his own world.

'Don't be long, lads. I wanna get to town,' says Carol.

Gordon grabs her and gives her a kiss. 'Twenty minutes and we're sorted,' he says. 'Keep the engine running. It's bloody freezing.'

Get rid, their father had said. Up country. Somewhere quiet, somewhere isolated. Bury him, then scarper. And no fucking monkey business. When they saw the slag heap out near Ashington it seemed the perfect place. Who's going to look for a corpse up there? Gordon gives the sack a firm kick where he thinks the head is. It gives off a hard, bony crack against his toe cap.

'Pack it in, Gogs.'

'Got better things to be doing on a Friday night. Fuck this.'

A heavy rain begins to fall.

'Let's get it done.'

They drag the sack through spiky scrubland, over ditches and through streams. A straggle of willows gives them respite from the rain for a while. It smells of moss and rotting bark. Jackdaws flap and squabble above them. They haul it over a stile and walk to the foot of the slag heap and stand in the gloom, among nettles, straining their necks. Frank checks his torch, shines it in Gordon's face.

'Piss off, will ya?'

They haul the sack up the shifting slag. It's as high as a mountain. Frank slips and falls and the sack rolls away into murk and he clambers back down, cursing, to find it and drag it back through the gathering sea fret. It's grey on grey on black. The stench of coal and tar fills his head. His boots sink in the rivers of grey sluice that run off the hill.

'Let's just dump the fucker,' Gordon shouts.

Frank ignores him. It's hard to find purchase under foot. His lips are caked. He spits a gobful of phlegm, black as bitumen. Progress is foot by foot and his thigh muscles burn. He ploughs on, head bent into the weather, his eyes narrowed against the rain. His hair is lank and wet, his fingers blistered and cut where he's stumbled and fallen against the clinker. Here and there a few patches of scrub and thistle grow where the National Coal Board has sown seeds in the vain hope of shoring up the structure, of laying down some root stock. Nothing can grow here. When at last they get to the top, they stand panting. It's nearly dark and they hug each other. When the clouds part, Frank studies the sodden hills. In the distance, the snowy peaks of the Cheviots glimmer. To their right the North Sea rolls like treacle, black and sluggish on the empty beaches. It gives no light back. The slag on which they stand glows bluely in the gloom, a dirty shade of amethyst. Colliery lights shine below. He sees the towering headstocks, stark and angular against the darkening fields. The great Victorian wheels turn silently. Deep within, the cages would be falling. The miners ready with their picks and bait boxes. All up the coast the lights of pit villages shine like cheap necklaces. He envies them their comfort, their fires in the hearths, their Christmas trees and flickering TV sets. Gordon lifts a finger and points. Tucked in a hollow a mile or two away are the multicoloured lights of a carousel, the Ferris wheel and dodgems of a distant fair. It shimmers like a mirage.

'Hot dogs,' says Gordon.

A thousand chimneys billow black into more black, so that everything grows vague. The clouds recall their congregations and the storm comes in off the sea, wiping everything from sight.

'Let's do it,' says Gordon.

Their shovels swim in the shifting waste. They dig a hole and it fills back in. Like digging a grave in the sea. They dig and dig but make no headway. The slag falls off their shovels like silt. Gordon tries to light a cigarette, but can't get a flame off his matches.

'Fuck this,' he shouts, and lifts the shovel high above his head, bringing it down with a savage blow. It slices through the sacking and into bone, splitting the fabric, throwing the contents of the bag open to the elements. It's Eddie Armstrong, his face staring at the sky, astounded by the sight. Frank lets out a shriek and brings his shovel down hard against the face and Gordon follows suit and they batter it. When they've finished, exhausted and breathless they look at the mess they've made.

'Fuck,' says Frank.

'Can't dig in this shit.'

'We might have to leave him, Gogs.'

'We'll have to take the fucking head off then.'

They stand for a moment. A blizzard of sleet blows off the sea, sharp as razors in the bitter wind. Malign and vicious. Frank senses Gordon has had enough, and sure enough, his brother lifts the haft of his shovel and with three quick strikes of the blade, takes off the head.

'Jesus, Gogs.'

'What?'

'Fucking Eddie.'

They stand in the downpour and look at him, sleet fizzing on their shoulders. Frank feels his stomach churn. He lost it there, for a moment. *What's Eddie done?* he wonders. It was only last Saturday they were stood on the terraces together, singing like lunatics. He bends for the severed head and picks it up by the hair.

'Let's get out of here,' he says, finally.

Frank nudges his brother and they lope off, down the slope. He can feel his legs sink into the sludge, ankle deep. The whole hill is a swamp.

At the bottom they gather themselves and look back up at the mass of unsteady mine waste. It looks like it could all come down in an instant. When they get to the car Frank settles Eddie's head on the bonnet and they light up cigarettes. Between each drag, Frank casts a glance at the battered face.

Carol gets out of the car to join them.

'Jesus Christ, Gordon.'

She looks at Frank for an explanation, but he shrugs his shoulders.

'Don't fucking ask, Caz.'

'It's Eddie,' says Gordon, with a snigger.

'Eddie Armstrong?'

'Yeah. It's fucking out of order,' Frank says, and blows a lungful of smoke into the chill air.

'I feel sick,' she says, turning away. 'Why would you do that?'

The front of the Vauxhall looks like the prow of a Viking ship, savage and terrifying. They stand in a bitter wind, studying the scene. Frank wonders what calamity must have brought this down on him. Eddie was one of their own. One of Dad's brokers. A hand in the till, probably. No bigger crime in the eyes of Laurence. Poor bastard. Gordon takes a last gasp on his butt end and flicks it into the bushes in a welter of sparks.

'Where's your shovel?' asks Frank.

'Fuck,' says Gordon. 'I left it up top.'

'You're gonna have to go back.'

Gordon laughs.

'I mean it,' says Frank.

But Frank sees that look in Gordon's eyes that means it's he, Frank, who will have to go back up. That nothing in the known world will get Gordon to climb that hill for a shovel. Frank sighs.

'You dick.'

He looks back at the mass of shifting waste and swears it's whispering to him.

—

They drive back to Newcastle in high spirits, through the dark and busy corridor of the A1, the tail lights glaring red against the onrush of white headlights in the mizzle and spray of a dirty, winter's night in Northumberland. The road top shines. Gordon is driving and Frank is sat beside him. Carol is in the back. The head is stowed in the boot. A half bottle of Bell's is being passed around, one to the other, as the radio, in festive mood is blasting out the old favourites: Slade, Sweet, Showaddywaddy. Saturday night and the pleasures of the Bigg Market await, another night mortal, birds and booze and a couple of bottle fights. Carol is leaning forwards against the driver's seat, her arms around Gordon's neck, singing along to 'Merry Xmas Everybody'. Occasionally, she lifts her hands and puts them over his eyes for a second or two, and Gordon lets out a scream as he goes blind, and then she lets go and the two of them howl with laughter. Frank is unimpressed.

'Pack it in, you two.'

She does it again and Gordon swerves the car left and right as if he's lost control and Frank grips the dashboard.

'We're all gonna die,' screams Gordon, and Carol screams too, and Gordon turns to Frank with a big grin on his face, overjoyed at his big brother's discomfort.

'You wanna drive, Frank?' he asks. 'I can get in the back with Caz.' He laughs, and Carol lets out a salacious snort. She's half-pissed now.

'Just concentrate, Gogs.'

'I can find my way home blindfolded, don't worry about that.'

'I do worry.'

'You're a laugh a fucking minute, mate.'

'We fucked up, back there.'

'Who gives a shit?'

'You will, when Laurence gets to hear.'

'Frank, relax.'

'We need to sort out the head before we hit town?'

Carol giggles.

'It's not funny, Caz.'

Gordon hits the brakes and everyone jolts forwards in their seats.

'What's that in the road ahead?'

'What?'

Gordon cracks into laughter. 'Ahead. A head. It's a joke, Frank.'

He drives on, smoking a cigarette, chuckling to himself.

'You coming in the back, Gordy?'

Gordon looks across at Frank with a hopeful, pleading look.

'Alright, pull in at the next services and we can swap.'

In the harsh, white glare of florescent lights they look like ghosts, except for Carol's bright red hair. They sit at a table overlooking the central reservation drinking tea and smoking cigarettes, watching the mindless flow of traffic, a plate of chips in front of each, daubed in ketchup and brown sauce. Frank looks around at the plastic furniture, the lino and filthy carpet. Depressing. Frank studies the two of them through a fog of smoke; a mixture of Park Drive, No 6, and Sobranie Cocktail. Gordon is gazing off down the dual carriageway, towards Newcastle, pumped up for a skinful with his mates no doubt. Frank wonders why his brother doesn't understand how important this is to their father. Maybe he does, but just refuses to accept it. Perhaps if Laurence didn't treat him like shit all the time, he'd feel more invested. Gordon turns to look at him across the grey Formica top. He stubs his cigarette out in the sugar bowl.

'It's just some dead guy, Frank. No one knows who it is. We've got the head. Just one more missing cunt who met with a tragic end.'

'I wish it was that easy.'

'It's Saturday night. Let's get home and hit the town.'

He reaches out and takes his brother's hand, squeezes it, then pulls Carol in with his other hand to kiss her.

'Me, you and Caz,' he says with a grin, 'we're a team,' and for once, he seems genuinely happy.

Outside, Gordon jumps on Frank's back and Frank carries him across the carpark. He brays like a donkey, staggering in the dark, the two of them, howling with laughter, back and forth, Gordon whipping him on the backside with his free hand.

'We swapping drivers, Frank?' he asks as his brother dumps him on the wet bonnet.

'Yeah. I'll drive us back.'

Frank has the music turned up loud, to smother the grunts and groans; the two of them making out in the back seat. He glances now and then in the mirror, but looks away. It kills him, the sound of her, the noise of her ministrations and attentions. How has it come to this? Why's it not him in the back with Carol, and Gordon driving them home? These are the roles they've been assigned, it seems; written in the ledger: Frank the sensible one, Gordon the joker, the loose cannon, the one who gets the girl, the one having all the fun, while he just thinks and worries.

He drops them off at the station. Gordon pops his head through the window once he's out.

'Lend us a fiver, Frank. I'm fucking skint.'

He slips a note from his wallet and hands it over. He watches them disappear into the night, then heads off, towards the coke ovens where their uncle Brendan works among the conflagration. The ovens never stop; they blister the night sky with alchemical flame and blazing magmas, turning coal into coke for the steelworks. A maelstrom that scours each night the very stars from the sky and during the day, creates vast, billowing cloudscapes. He drives on, into the orange-coloured world ahead of him, the rain still sluicing down. When he gets there he finds his uncle standing naked to the waist in front of the ovens. One of the legendary oven killers, his job to tame the furnace, to quench the flames at the process end. To drown it in water, sending a tumult of scalding steam into the air. These men are of a different kind. Working in Hades, forever singed, breathing in the noxious coke fumes.

Brendan greets him with a broad, happy grin, his brother's eldest come for a favour. He slaps him on the back and takes the sack from Frank.

'Don't worry,' Brendan shouts above the din, 'there's always someone coming down here wi sommat to get rid of.'

He approaches an oven and opens one of the doors to hell. Frank sees inside, the roiling incandescence. He throws in the bag. It glows for the briefest moment, then disappears in a puff. His uncle is vast and covered in sweat. It runs off his face and down his heavy shoulders, his thick arms. He closes the door and gives Frank a hug.

'Best regards to our kid,' he says, with a deep voice and a big guffaw. Frank is in awe of the man. So different from their father, so full of generosity. You'd never think them brothers.

He wanders back to his car and sits a while in silence, then drives down to the riverside. It is high tide and the Tyne is swollen, turbulent. He can smell the sea through the open window. He watches the current. It seems angry, but maybe that's him. He thinks about Eddie, what a good bloke he was. He watches the swirl and swell of the river, and through the open window, he can hear the water suck at the dark wharves.

sierra de cádiz 2003

Frank drives up the dirt track between two mountains, the villa above him perched on an outcrop of rock. The exiled king in his eyrie. Frank is curious to see his brother's palaces, his plunder, the riches of his kingdom, though he has to admit: he's a little scared. He can scarcely believe he's found the place. Twenty-five years and not a word between them. He can see the occasional flash of sunlight as binoculars are lifted and dropped. He's being watched. Typical of his paranoid younger brother. It's not an easy drive. He has to be wary of potholes and landslip and the loose gravelled surface. Eventually he pulls up in front of the villa; white like every other villa in Andalusia, well appointed, grand. It's cool in the car. He switches off and lets it settle. He sees his brother for the first time in decades, peering through the tinted windows. Dressed in overalls, unbuttoned to the waist, a wrench of some kind in his hand. Frank takes a moment to study him; spitting image of the old man, but stockier. He's put on weight. Double chin. Grey-haired. Frank opens the door and steps out into the furnace. The white of the villa is blinding.

'Gogs,' he says, and holds out a hand. He can feel his heart pounding.

His brother looks stunned, and when he finally takes his hand, Frank grips it and pulls him in. They hug for a moment, awkwardly, then stand apart, sizing each other up.

'I've been expecting you,' says Gordon.

'Have you? That surprises me.'

'Every morning I open the curtains and think: *I wonder if they're coming for me today.* I never thought they'd send you.'

'It's not that, Gordon.'

'No?'

'You're my brother.'

'I remember,' says Gordon.

Frank looks around him, the villa, the pool, a car port with an old American motor on blocks, its bonnet up. He wipes the sweat off his forehead with a shirt sleeve and Gordon stands before him in the searing sun. Thou shalt not pass.

'Can we get in the shade, mate? I'm burning up here.'

His brother nods and goes towards the car.

'I'll get your bags,' he says.

As Frank walks towards the villa there's a gasp of delight from beneath the grapevines that cover the patio.

'Frankie. My God!'

Carol runs towards him in a black bikini and flip-flops, her mouth in a broad smile. Still that mass of red hair. He can see his own face in the mirrored lenses of her sunglasses. She beams like a teenager as she grasps and hugs him. The heat of her body. He smells the perfume, familiar still; it hasn't changed in a quarter century. It takes him back home, the terraces of Wallsend. He sees it momentarily, like a Polaroid. All the faded colours. He extricates himself and stands back to see her more clearly: darkly burnished by the sun, healthy, no more that pasty Tyneside complexion. She looks good. A few fine lines around the eyes, but life in Spain must suit her. He notes the wedding ring. The piercings are long gone. Not even an earring.

'Christmas Carol. Look at you!'

She looks across at Gordon, then pulls away.

'Frankie,' she says, then dashes back in the house.

'Something I said?' he asks, turning to Gordon.

'Time of the month. You know what birds are like.'

Frank winces and studies his brother for a moment.

'What?' asks Gordon.

'Nowt.'

He looks around him again; the land, the house, the pool.

'Nice place you've got here.'

'I earned it,' says Gordon.

'Never said you didn't.'

'Just saying.'

'It's alright, Gogs, I haven't come to cause trouble.'

Frank can hear the cogs whirring in his brother's head. Showing up suddenly, all these years later. He's suspicious. He thinks Frank is here on business. Fair enough, he'd probably be the same. Gordon wanders over to his barbecue.

'Just about to fire her up,' he says, over his shoulder. 'You'll be wanting some grub.'

Frank watches him for a moment preparing the coals. Coarse, grey hair covers his upper back. Frank tries to see him as he used to be, when they were kids: lean and soulful and pale as pastry, bent over rock pools in Dunbar, a net in one hand and a bucket full of salty, red crabs in the other. Now he's bullnecked, beefy, all the signs of the good life, or the dissolute. A decent beer gut, but you can't judge him for that.

He sees Carol through the window, rinsing glasses. He goes into the kitchen. The cool stone chills the sweat on his skin and he shivers. She stands with a glass in her hand watching him, the light from the window casting her in semi-shadow. Her russet hair glows, just like it used to. She looks away, out of the kitchen window.

'You alright, Carol?'

'I'm sorry, Frankie. I didn't think I'd ever see you again,' she says.

He looks at her in the dark of the kitchen. He looks back out of the door, at the blinding light. Then back to her, ghost that she is. He'd like to hug her again, but thinks better of it.

'It's good to see you,' he says.

'It's good to see you too, Frank.'

They stand a moment in awkward silence.

'You got any water in that fridge?'

Carol laughs and turns to open the door. She takes out a jug and puts it on the table. He sees the revolver beside the fruit bowl. Brutal in the soft light. He picks it up and looks it over. She shakes her head, takes a new glass from a shelf and puts it beside the jug.

'Redhawk .44,' he says.

'He took it out when he saw your car coming up the hill.'

'Paranoid?'

'Put it down, Frankie.'

He checks the cylinder, all six chambers full.

'Where the hell did he get this from?'

'Put it in the drawer, Frank. It makes me nervous.'

He spins the cylinder. So clean. The little clicks and ticks of its mechanism. Beautiful. He lets it lie in the flat of his hand for a moment. Feels its weight. Must be nearly four pounds. This is no gangster's gun. He opens the drawer. It's full of cartridges. A slovenly habit. He lays the revolver among them and closes the drawer. He hasn't touched a gun for decades. It makes his pulse race. Too much bloodshed. Too much suffering. He pours himself a glass. The water is so cold, it burns.

The room they give him is cool and fragrant. It faces west with a view down the coast: hillsides littered with white villages. Through the open window the scent of jasmine comes in on the breeze. A bland and nondescript bedroom, like a B&B back home. Perfect for a day or two. If he can last that long. He takes off his sweat-soaked shirt, his chinos and undies and stands in the shower, turns it on and lets the water sluice over him. Down here, even the cold is warm. Afterwards, by the window, his wet skin feels cool and refreshed against the breeze. He unzips his case, takes out his notebook, Lorca's poems and a copy of *Blood Wedding*. He puts them on the dresser beside the bed, shakes the creases out of a pair of shorts, a thin cotton shirt. His old university rugby shirt is folded neatly at the bottom of his case. He runs his thumb across the badge, the motto 'Fundamenta Super Montibus', and holds it to his face. It smells of the Tyne, dried as it was a hundred times in his grandmother's garden. He thinks about Gordon, the times they shared there, beside the river, fishing or messing about. He seems so tightly wound up. Poor Carol. He lies back on his bed and closes his eyes. He should never have come.

kelso - scotland 2002

The kirkyard is set within a grey stone wall, a small church built out of granite and slate. Tight as a fist. Beyond, the North Sea rolls in anger. A fine spray falls on everything. His father insisted on being buried. A pain in the arse, but it makes sense to Frank. A box full of ashes seems to lack all sense of gravitas. So, here they are, dropping him in a hole on the Scottish borders with a quarter-tonne headstone to top it all off. This is where *his* old man was buried, in the pissing rain, the sodden turf, the scruffy-looking gorse. He studies the mourners, stood in various clusters, rubbing their hands in the bitter breeze. All the useless hangers-on, the cap-doffers, the bought-off coppers, local politicians and businessmen, pathetic. They'd all despised Laurence, and he'd despised them, most of them. Once upon a time big, important people, dwindled now to the old and ineffectual. How that must hurt. Frank moves off to the rear, waiting. What would he read, this bald-headed, meek-looking vicar with the whisky tremor in his voice? The man bows his head, and speaks, as if addressing the soil itself. Frank can hardly hear a word from where he's stood. The vicar does his ashes-to-ashes bit then snaps his Bible shut. It sounds like the last word, and the glum mourners scatter at last, for baps at the Cadogan.

Frank lingers a while and waits. He's surprised to see a woman walk out of nowhere and stand beside the grave. It's Carol's younger sister. He can't believe it. She smiles with a smile from decades ago. He's so happy to see her. They hug against the cold wind.

'Frank.'

'Dawn.'

'I'm sorry about your dad.'

They stand for a while, in silence, as the gulls keep up their pitiful cries. She turns to look at him.

'We all thought you were dead,' she says.

'The resurrection of Frank Bridge,' he says, and wants to laugh, but it feels inappropriate. 'I've been around,' he says, and fills her in on some of it: Spain mainly, early on, then back here, keeping his head down, studying, avoiding this place, these people.

'I was so happy when I heard you'd turned up again.'

'Just in time. He'd well near lost his marbles by the time I found him, dribbling in that shithole. I wasn't really sure he knew who I was.'

She has a single white rose in her hand and twirls it, absently.

'Chuck it in, if you want,' he says, gesturing at the grave before them. She laughs and lets it go. It tumbles down into the scattering of soil and other bouquets.

'Spain, you said.'

'Yeah, for a good while.'

'Do you see your brother?'

'In Spain?'

'I just wondered.'

'I haven't seen Gordon in twenty-odd years. No one knows what happened to him.'

'I know where he is.'

He turns to her with astonishment.

'What?'

'I do,' she says, with a grin.

'They looked all over the place. No one found him.'

'Well, they'd have to know where to look, wouldn't they.'

She takes a biro from her bag and scribbles something on the back of a cheque book. She tears it off and hands it to Frank. He reads it and smiles. Typical. Where else? The land is vast and mountainous there, folded and refolded like a crumpled crisp packet. No wonder they couldn't find him. He reads it again and laughs at the irony. In Spain. All this bloody time. He slips the address into his wallet.

'So, you've seen them. How is he? How's Carol?'

She looks away over the gravestones off towards the moors.

'I don't really know. I wish I did.' She pauses again. 'It's Gordon,' she says, at last. 'It's difficult. I'm not welcome there any more.'

Frank waits for some kind of elucidation, but none is forthcoming. If she wants to say more, she will.

'The last time I saw you, Gordon was driving away with all the cash,' he says.

'I'll never forget it.'

'Strange how things turn out, how everything falls into place, in retrospect. It all makes sense in a funny way. Back then it was different. It seemed like the end of the world.'

'They weren't nice times, Frank.'

'I don't know, Dawn. Things are what they are. What they're meant to be.'

He'd given up hope of ever seeing Gordon again, and now, just like that, he finds him, on the day of his father's funeral. It's like a miracle. He looks out to sea. Spindrift. The finest sea spray against his face. An invigorating day.

'It's good to see you, Frank. I better go. If you do see them, tell Carol I miss her.'

Frank nods, then hugs her and watches her out of the churchyard. He feels a twinge of sadness, some strong lure pulling from the past. This is how it touches you, he thinks: with bitterness, and a touch of cynicism.

He looks around as solitude sweeps in, resuming its brutal ministry. It's like nothing has happened here for centuries, save the diggers digging a hole by the wall. The sound of the slops on their spade heads, a laugh, some incoherent grumble. Someone will come along later and do the stonework. He'll probably never see it now, but he's paid for it. He looks at his mother's stone, stout and solid beside his father's grave. He lays his own bouquet on her grave and stands for a moment, remembering her. Thirty years have passed. What an almighty fuck-up. The loneliness is palpable: the low-slung moors fading off into grey, primordial fog. Land of his fathers, desolate, grim, but with a ruthless beauty, if you have the heart for it. A malevolent, tireless wind blows in from Scandinavia, scrubbing the names off the headstones. He wanders around, looking at them. Blank, each one. Who knows who's buried here? Unless you remember doing it yourself, they remain unnumbered and lost. It brings to mind Lorca, as ever: *If death is death, what will become of the poets and of sleeping things, that no one remembers?* Lichen grows in a rich, cuneiform script, grey, green, even blue, across the gnarled slabs. A language of its own making, understood by no one. The headstones lean at various, incongruous angles, precarious, teetering it seems, though anchored solidly in clay. His father. Gone for good. All that hard graft. King of the Tyne. Export fraud, extortion, murder, trafficking, contraband. There wasn't a dock owner or shipper he didn't know, who he didn't have in his pocket. Easy access to the high seas, the Middle East, the Americas. All those hard men, the crowbars and shotguns. The corpses. No one stood up to him, and so he walked all over the lot of them. A long and pointless life.

Frank shakes his head. He was lucky to get out. He turns and jumps the wall and walks the beach, a mile or so into the wind. Head down, his coat pulled tight around him. So, now he can go to Gordon. Give him the news, see him again after all this time. He pulls up his collar. The wind is fearsome and a sudden rain batters his coat, but he pushes on, like a penitent, the white noise of the surf hissing around him.

wallsend - newcastle 1972

Searching for Gordon and finding him nowhere, Frank opens the door of his parents' bedroom. He finds his brother on the edge of the bed stroking his mother's hand. Frank halts. What is he doing? She lies inert, her eyes closed, a small bubble or two on her pale lips.

'Jesus, Gogs,' he says, and Gordon looks up at him from a great distance. He seems mesmerised. Frank sees the blister packs strewn across the carpet, their little moons of foil glimmering, and it dawns on him. He pulls his brother off and sits beside her. He takes her hand and speaks to her.

'Mam, it's Frank.' She is far away and drifting. He shivers in the cold of the bedroom, the windows open to the winter chill. His father likes sleeping in the subzero. It's good for the chest, apparently. The whole house is chill as a fridge, except for the back room where they eat and watch TV, where the gas fire's enduring hiss is the one constant.

Now though, their mother is laid on the eiderdown, cold as a corpse. Her breath comes fitfully. He leans in to hear, to feel its warmth on his cheek. Her grip is weak, barely a grip at all.

'Mam.'

Frank is scared. There's no reply. What can he ask? How many? When? How long ago? He asks Gordon instead. He found her after school, he says, which was four, and now it is nearly six. He needs to fetch Dad, phone the ambulance.

He gets up to go, but his mother senses his departure, grasps his wrist and lets out some pitiful dog whine. He yanks his arm away.

'Look after her,' he says, and heads downstairs to the phone as Gordon takes up vigil, holding her hand in the mausolean chill.

—

Laurence kicks open the bedroom door, Frank at his heels. Laurence grabs Gordon by his collar and throws him to the floor. You stupid bastard, he shouts; at Gordon, or at their mother, it's impossible to tell. Gordon is curled against the skirting where his father has thrown him. And Laurence is on her. Mouth to mouth which frightens Frank, and Gordon too begins to wail. Their father slaps her face, four, five times. He is trying to wake her.

'How long has she been like this? When did you find her?' he barks at his son. He scoops up a handful of Xanax cartons off the bedside cabinet, looks at them briefly, crumples them and throws them on the carpet in disgust. 'How fucking long?'

Gordon shakes his head and turns towards the wall. The lights of an ambulance are flashing against the closed curtains. Laurence stands and turns from the bed and rushes down the stairs to the front door, rushes back up and sends the boys downstairs, to keep out of the fucking way. Frank and Gordon sit at the backroom table. Soon the medics are wheeling their mother on a gurney through the house. Will she make it? Laurence wants to know.

'Are you the lad that found her?' the medic asks Gordon, and Gordon nods.

'When was this?'

'I dunno.'

Laurence is shaking his head.

'Was it after school, before?'

'I just got in from school,' he says. 'She was already asleep.'

'Jesus fucking H,' mutters Laurence. 'It's gone half six now, you daft bastard.'

Gordon flinches. 'I didn't know what to do,' he says to the face of the medic.

The medic smiles. 'Do you know how many pills she took?'

He doesn't know.

'There's a tonne of boxes all over the bedroom floor,' says Laurence.

'We need to get her to the general.'

Laurence is pacing. 'How fucking long were you sat

there, holding her hand and doing precisely nowt?' he wants to know.

'It's not my fault,' says Gordon, 'I didn't do owt.'

'I know you didn't. That's why she's half fucking dead.'

Gordon bursts into tears.

Laurence is raging.

'Stupid fucking bitch.'

It's everyone's fault but his.

'I'll come with you,' he tells the ambulance crew.

He turns back to the boys, his face contorted. 'Stop here and don't move a fucking muscle. Got that?'

'Yes.'

Gordon cradles his head on the dining-room table, sobbing.

'I was just holding her hand.'

Frank is sat silently by, holding back tears, a rising anger inside of him, but an anger he can't fix on any one thing; on his mother, on his father, on the wider world beyond.

—

It's late when Gran arrives from the hospital, distraught, tear-stained. She hugs the boys as the gas fire hisses its admonishment. She has a handkerchief bunched up in her fist. They sit at the table and wait. Gran is stroking Gordon's head.

'That man,' she says. 'That bloody man.'

'What man?' Gordon wants to know.

'Such a monster.'

They sit, like card players dealing their final hands, resolved to losses beyond their reckoning.

'It's the kidneys. That's what does for them,' Gran announces, although the utterance is merely self-assuaging, a kind of grim prolepsis.

When Laurence returns, he's despondent, more taciturn that usual.

'They've kept her in. She's in a very bad way.'

He smokes tab after tab, stubbing them out in an aluminium ashtray until the room is thick.

Under his gran's guidance, Gordon has taken to knitting his football scarf, black and white stripes, already two feet long. His pride and joy. The mighty Magpies, Supermac, John Tudor, Terry Hibbitt. It seems to calm him. Laurence glares. Frank can see how it riles his father and he wishes Gordon would put it away, for now. Sure enough, Laurence can hide his disgust no longer. He rises from his chair and grabs the knitting out of Gordon's hands, tears the wool from the needles and throws them on the hearthrug.

'You fucking pansy.'

Gordon is screaming now and Gran is up on her feet cursing Laurence, expletives Frank has never heard her utter before. He can see in her face the hatred she feels for the man. Frank wants to do something. To intervene. To calm things, but he feels paralysed. His father's hands are balled into fists, the way that Gordon's go when he

35

snaps and feels there's no more he can do. Finally their father turns, pulls on his coat again and leaves the house in a tirade of curses. They sit and listen as footsteps recede down the garden path, Frank's heart is pounding in his chest. Gran bends to retrieve the scarf. She holds it before her like some injured bird and studies it, tears running down her face.

sierra de cádiz 2003

Frank comes down and pulls a chair up to the patio table. He puts a broad-rimmed hat on his head to keep off the sun. There are bowls of olives, bottles of Rioja. Paper plates. Knives and forks in a Union Jack mug. Under the table is a bucket of beers on ice. Carol is tossing a green salad with wooden spoons.

'Grab a beer, Frank, there's plenty,' she says.

'I've given up the drink.'

Gordon turns to him, a look of incredulity on his face.

'Doctors orders,' says Frank, and he winks at Carol.

He has a seat in the shade, under the purple grapes. The scent of bougainvillea drifts in the air along with the sweet smell of charcoal. Carol goes back to the kitchen and returns with a bowl of tomatoes and lemons.

'My own lemons, Frank. Off the trees,' she says, with a touch of pride.

'Fucking lemons,' Gordon snorts. 'Where else they gonna grow?'

'*My* trees,' she insists, and swivels her eyes at Frank.

'I'd like to see those trees,' he says.

'I've got a lovely allotment,' she says, her voice perking

up, 'you'll be amazed what I'm growing. So many good things: tomatoes, courgettes, even pomegranates.'

'Pomegranates. Fuck them,' says Gordon, and spits on the coals. They give off a hiss. He takes a swig from his beer.

Frank watches him at the coals, prodding, husbanding. He pokes the charcoal with a tenderness that seems ridiculous. He remembers this goading and petty bickering from back in Newcastle. Always vile to each other, like a kind of game, he'd often thought. She'd come to him in tears from something he'd said or done, and then the next moment she'd be all over him. He could never understand it. Carol prepares the table. She catches him looking at her, and smiles. If Gordon is like this all the time it must be hell up here, all on their own. She heads back into the kitchen.

'Bring that fucking meat out,' he shouts at her.

Frank watches proceedings in silence and pours himself a glass of water from the jug. A minute later Carol brings out a plastic bag. It squirms with pink sausages. She drops them on the table beside his altarpiece. He forks them onto the grill. A neat, orderly row. He gropes about at the bottom of the bag and finds the burgers. There are greaseproof papers between each one. He peels them off like banknotes and lays the meat over the flame.

Frank considers asking for tea, but then thinks better of it. Soon the sausages are split and weeping. They smell good. Gordon takes some bread buns, pre-cut, from a bag and lays them out on the table, a bottle of HP sauce and a jar of Colman's stand by. He takes the sausages off the grill, and places them on the bread. He sauces and mustards and crowns each one with a bun top. He presses until they squeak, hands one to Frank and slides the other plate over to Carol with the first smile that Frank has seen him give her. It's Gordon's turn. Four sausages and a big dollop of Colman's. Frank watches him: stocky, uneasy on his feet. He stands and eats in a shroud of blue smoke. It disappears in a few bites. He wipes his mouth and takes a swig of lager. Must be warm by now. He rises and goes to stand by Gordon, gives him a gentle, affectionate punch on the shoulder. His brother flinches at the touch.

'There's no fucking money,' he says.

'I'm not interested in money.'

'Everyone's interested in money. They send you?'

'No one sent me, Gogs.'

Gordon shakes his head and turns to Frank. A look of disdain, contempt, or is it fear that Frank can see in his eyes?

'I came out here looking for someone,' he says, hoping a change of subject might calm things down. Gordon thinks it's gang business and perks up, briefly.

'Do I know 'em?'

Frank laughs. 'You never know. He's a poet. Was.'

'A what?'

'A poet.'

'Oh, I like poetry,' says Carol from her lounger.

Gordon spits on the coals again, adds more meat to the barbecue. Sweat pours off him. He glistens.

'Fuck you on about?'

'I'm writing a book about him.'

39

Gordon turns to Frank with a look of consternation.

'You're winding me up.'

'It's just a book, Gogs.'

Carol is delighted and claps her hands.

'You're so clever Frankie,' she says. 'Do you know some?'

'Some what?' says Frank.

'Some of his poems.'

'One or two.'

'Tell us one,' she says.

Frank looks across at his brother and thinks better of it. He shakes his head at her.

'Not right now, Carol.'

'Please, Frank.'

They're both looking at him, like they're waiting for a speech. A bead of sweat rolls down his nose. This is not the time for poetry.

'You driven down from Blighty in that?' asks Gordon, finally, nodding at the Merc.

'I drove it down from Córdoba,' says Frank, thankful for the change of subject.

'What you doing up there?'

'It's a long story.'

'Enlighten us. We got all day.'

Frank's shirt is sticking to him. His mouth is dry. *Christ, get it over with*, he thinks.

'It's Dad, Gogs,' he says eventually.

'What?'

'He's dead.'

Gordon looks dumbfounded. He murmurs something indecipherable. Frank watches him wipe his face with the full, flat palm of his hand. There's a nod of his head. His eyes narrow, then he turns around as if he hasn't heard a thing. He stares off across the campo. A vein pumps in Frank's temple: tick, tick. Above the patio, on a thin pole, a sun-bleached flag of St George hangs limp.

'Oh, I'm sorry,' says Carol, and it looks like she's overcome. Frank is surprised. She always despised Laurence for the way he treated Gordon, though Laurence had a soft spot for her. He respected her feistiness, her honourable nature. He always wished he'd had a daughter, he used to like telling people. *Instead I got two cunts called Frank and Gordon.*

She walks over to Gordon and throws her arms around him. For a moment he seems to soften, but then he pushes her away.

'Fuck off.'

It's barely a whisper. She stands her ground and glares at him, at his dripping, turned back, then she walks to Frank and hugs him. He takes her in his arms. He feels a great relief for a moment, and then his own tears arrive. He blinks them away, ashamed in part, but also pleased finally to let it out.

He goes over to Gordon.

'I'm sorry, Gogs.'

'And you can fuck off too,' he says, turning on Frank, the long barbecue-blackened fork shaking in his hand.

dunbar - scotland 1974

Whitsuntide, whatever that means. The schools are out and everyone heads to the coast; coachloads to Whitley Bay, South Shields, Bamburgh. Laurence takes the kids over the border, away from the riffraff. He likes to be among his own people, in Scotland, a few days camping in the usual place, east of Edinburgh.

Laurence is in the comfort of a static caravan, the boys in a tent. They lie under canvas, bored, fighting in the cramped space, the tent creaking against its guy-ropes and pegs, a tirade of expletives and foul language upsetting the retirees, relaxing in their deck chairs. Frank hates it. As far as he can tell everyone hates it and always has. The boredom. The trudge to the farm shop for eggs, milk and sausages for breakfast. The cold shower blocks, the stench of Calor gas drifting between the pitches. Sometimes the sun shines, but mostly a thin, grey drizzle blows. They play snap, in the caravan if Laurence permits it. They take their meals there too: beans on toast, Campbell's meatballs and tinned peas, or if it's fine out, then under the awning attached to the door of the caravan. They do the washing-up, they wash the car, they wash the caravan. Still, it's better than school, though they miss their mates.

This year there are girls in one of the tents. Two Scottish girls, students from Glasgow. This is a turn up. They're good-looking. They sit by the sea in bikinis, a tape recorder blaring out rock music: guitars and keyboards, mysterious, ethereal sounds. Hippies, their father calls them, bloody hippies.

Frank and Gordon spend the days gazing at them from behind the thick tufts of marram grass on the sand dunes, hiding as best they can. One afternoon, while their father is off conducting business from a payphone up on the A1, they find the girls smoking among the dunes. One of them calls the two spies down. They're shy now, intimidated, but intrigued enough to brave it. Frank watches, fascinated as one of the girls sprinkles tobacco into her cigarette papers, adds deep green leaves on top and rolls up the biggest cigarette Frank has ever seen. It must be marijuana.

'You want some?' she asks.

'What is it?'

'Spliff.'

'Spliff,' says Gordon.

'What's that?' asks Frank.

Both the girls laugh.

'I'll have some,' says Gordon.

'Sure,' says the girl. 'Just don't tell your dad. OK?'

He shuffles up beside her and she hands Gordon the spliff. He takes a drag and coughs. Frank is watching, intently.

'Take it slowly,' she says. 'And deeply. Hold it there until you feel light and relaxed, then blow it all out.'

He does so, and when he blows it out finally, he lies back, laughing. He looks at his brother.

'Bloody hell.'

The girl offers it to Frank, and he takes it, inhaling deeply. He holds it as long as he can, then blows it out as the beach turns upside down. He lets out a gasp and hangs on tight.

'Fuck.'

His stomach churns. He hears someone ask if he's OK. He feels how he feels after a night on the waltzers and the big dipper at the fair. He holds his stomach. His head is dizzy, and he feels nauseous. He gets up and staggers. He clambers up the dune to find somewhere to be sick. On the other side, in the cooling breath of the ocean, he gets down on his haunches and breathes in deeply, trying to clear his head. He pukes in the sand at the base of the dune. He covers it up, then rolls over and lies on his back. He watches the clouds drift overhead, sharp as cut glass.

When he clambers back to the others, he finds Gordon face to face with one of the girls. She has the lighted end of the spliff in her mouth and is blowing hard. The smoke pours out of the other end, into Gordon's mouth. He falls back in the sand as if someone has punched him in the face, but curled up with giggles.

'Shotgun,' she says, to Frank. 'You want a go?'

Frank shakes his head.

'I don't think it agrees with me.' He watches them smoke. He's never seen girls so captivating.

'What's the weird music?'

'*Ummagumma.*'

'What's that?'

'Pink Floyd.'

'I don't know what that is,' he says, and the girls laugh at him.

'What do you listen to?'

'Quo. Thin Lizzy.'

They nod their heads. 'Too heavy, that. We prefer Floyd with a spliff, or Joni Mitchell.'

Gordon is laughing at every word.

'Your brother is stoned,' says one of the girls with a snigger.

'I'm stoned,' says Gordon, and Frank laughs too.

'He doesn't even know what he's talking about.'

After a while, the girls get up to go. They're heading into Edinburgh to have a good time.

'Do you want to come along?'

'We can't. Dad will be back soon,' says Frank.

The girls wander off, and he and Gordon lie there in the sand, dizzy and stunned.

'I'm stoned, Frank.'

'Yeah, I guess so. Dad will bloody well knock your head off.'

'I know,' he says, and cracks up again, as if he's just heard the joke of the century.

The next morning the girls are gone and Frank is

devastated. There's just a pale green rectangle where the tent had been. They stand there, looking at the ghost of the groundsheet.

'Fuck it.'

'Yeah.'

Frank walks off and stands beyond the dunes, at the sea's edge. He's taken from the girls some vague, but powerful sense of freedom, something he longs for but cannot grasp, or articulate. He envies his brother's independence. Always his own man. He does things his way, even if it gets him into trouble. Frank realises, that in spite of all his thoughtfulness, his grand imaginings, Gordon has more freedom than he ever will.

Sunday is their last day. They're preoccupied with crabs in the rock pools: the way they scuttle over the rocks, or drift in slow motion over the sandy floors. Gordon has a bucket full. The brightest and most fearsome. They hear Laurence bellowing from somewhere down the beach. He shouts their names against the ravening sea, his voice deep and loud, even here, out of doors, under the endless sky. They rise from their endeavours and walk along the beach towards their father. They spend a while walking the tideline, 'taking the air' as Laurence has it. 'A constitutional.' He holds the boys' hands, one each side and Frank feels an acute embarrassment at such unusual, fatherly affection. What's got into him? He clings on tight for fear of breaking this fragile peace.

'Breathe in deep,' advises Laurence, 'the air is a tonic.'

The two of them rush ahead as the sea washes in

and they dodge the edges of the waves, emitting playful screams as Laurence cautions them against the wet sand and the incoming tide, telling them to watch their new shoes, and to stop acting the fucking goat. They have to get back to Newcastle soon. He has to be back for the club.

'I want to put the crabs back,' says Gordon, walking them over towards the rocks.

Each pool is a chest of sunken treasures, full of colourful gems and stones and animated life: starfish, anemones. Tiny fry twitch and flicker like iron shavings, and as the tide advances ribbons of dark, green seaweed tremble in the current.

Frank lifts a small green crab from the sandy floor of the pool and shows it to Laurence. It seems to change colour as he turns it in his hand, first green, then blue, then pink.

'Nacreous,' his father says, which means nothing to Frank.

He studies the shell, then drops it back in the water. Gordon lifts another crab and holds it out in front of him. It has vivid, red eyes. He holds it by a leg and lets it dangle before his eyes. He seems rapt. What is it, he wonders.

Laurence tells him it's a devil crab, that it likes to snap. Gordon holds it up, sniggering. 'Devil crab,' he repeats and pokes at the coppery claw. When it snaps at him, he shrieks and drops it on the rocks with a clatter.

Laurence laughs again, but Gordon slips on some seaweed and falls headfirst into the pool. Frank churns out a belly laugh and Gordon comes up gasping.

'Fucking crab,' he spits, laughing too.

Laurence erupts. He grabs Gordon by the scruff and hauls him up, his clothes dripping. He slaps him in the face and Gordon flinches and pushes him back, so that Laurence too slips, falls off the rocks onto the sand. He's on his hands and knees. Frank can't believe it and braces for the consequences, but Gordon has picked up his bucket and is off down the beach, wiping his nose on the back of his hand, cursing into the wind.

Laurence struggles to his feet, dusting the sand off his suit, watching his son storm off down the beach.

'I'll skin you alive, you little runt.'

He bends over then, out of breath, hyperventilating.

Frank sees him gasping and goes to him.

'You alright, Dad?'

'I'll skin him.'

'Let him alone.'

Laurence pulls up and stares at his son.

'You what?'

'It was accident. Leave him alone.'

Frank's heart is pounding. He holds his father's arm. He can feel the tense muscles move under his grip. Full of anger. And then the energy goes out of him. He looks at his son, bewildered. Frank has never seen this in his eyes before. A kind of resignation, of something like surrender. Laurence turns and strolls off towards the car. Frank watches him go and notices how small he seems, how suddenly frail. His father's anger seems all out of proportion, and now he's terrified himself, for speaking out like that. Where did it come from? Frank wanders down the beach to find Gordon. He's sitting on a rock, hugging his knees, looking out to sea. Has he been crying? His knuckles are bleeding. He's pulled all the legs off a crab, and has bashed its shell against the rock. It lies shattered on the sand. Frank picks it up and shakes his head.

'What?'

'Nowt,' says Frank.

'Well fuck off then.'

Frank climbs up and sits, and puts his arm around him. They sit a while, in silence, watching seabirds struggle in the wind, dogs bolting up and down the beach. Frank looks at Gordon's shoes, sodden, crusted in sand. He laughs. Gordon takes them off and looks at them, one after the other.

'They're alright,' says Frank.

'They're fine.'

'It's not about shoes.'

'What is it about?'

'What do you think?'

'I dunno. He just fucking hates me. That's all.'

'He hates everyone, Gogs.'

'Not you.'

Frank can't answer that. Maybe he does.

'I don't know.'

'You don't know much.'

Frank laughs. 'No. I don't.'

'Well, I hate him,' says Gordon.

'I don't blame you.'

50

'I miss Mam.'

'I know. Me too.'

'He still thinks it's my fault.'

'Well fuck him, Gogs.'

Frank feels invigorated, charged up. He felt a brief power over his father just now. A deliverance of sorts, which he can't quite define. The world seems suddenly more plentiful.

'You fancy a swim, Gogs?'

They slip off the rocks, chuck off their jackets and shirts and vests, their trousers and socks. They stand in nylon underpants beneath a tepid sun, clasp each other momentarily, clammy and slick as seals, then make a dash into the bitter, cold North Sea.

sierra de cádiz 2003

By late afternoon, the atmosphere is intolerable. The heat too; things pop and crack in the tinder-dry descampado surrounding the villa. Frank guesses the area was farmed once, but the trees are wild now, unruly in their growth. They haven't been pruned in decades, but they cling on tight and flourish in spite of the drought. Gordon floats in the swimming pool, Frank can hear him cursing. They keep their own counsel as the afternoon wears on. Siesta time, though nothing stops for the boozing. Frank wonders if he could live like this. How bored he would get. He thinks of Lorca down in the Huerta in Granada, his summer home, writing in his cool room overlooking wheat fields. Gordon clambers out of the pool again. He just can't settle. He stands on the patio, dripping. Carol stirs herself and goes to the kitchen. She comes back with a bottle of sherry and puts it on the table. Things seem to be calming down.

'I'm sorry we missed the funeral,' says Carol.

'It wasn't much of a funeral. Just a bunch of losers. The usual hangers-on, all knackered now, decrepit. I'd have let you know, of course, but I had no idea where you were.'

'And now you do,' Gordon spits. 'How come?' He turns to Carol. 'That bitch sister of yours?'

Carol shrugs.

'He got it from somewhere,' he says.

Gordon sits on a stool and empties his glass, puts his elbows on his knees and bows his head. He gobs on the ground. Frank watches it darken the flagstones, then evaporate and disappear.

'Well, he can rot in hell.'

'Don't say that, Gordon.'

'Fuck you.'

'Give it a rest, Gogs,' says Frank.

Gordon turns on him with a look of fury. 'Telling me what to do? In my own fucking house? Fuck you, Frank. Just piss off back home with your bullshit.'

Carol gets to her feet and marches towards Gordon, her face crimson. Full of rage. Frank watches on, helpless.

'Is that how you speak? You own brother. Your dead father? You're a vile, ungrateful slob.'

'You what?' says Gordon.

He gets to his feet, half-stumbling.

'Look at yourself,' she says. 'Nothing but a wasted drunk. So full of hate and bitterness.'

He turns on her, his face contorted. For a moment it seems like he's going to punch her, but then he turns, full of exasperation, and kicks over a plastic chair. It skitters awkwardly across the flags into the pool.

'What do you know about it?' he says.

'I just know you're a mean, selfish bastard,' says Carol.

He turns, and once more walks up to her, but she stands her ground. Immobile, implacable.

'Go on then,' she says.

He lifts his hand and grips her face, her two cheeks clamped tight in his grip. He pushes her backwards and her shades go flying. She staggers and falls against the barbecue with a scream. Frank rises and goes towards her.

'Carol.'

Her sunglasses curl and blacken on the barbecue, then pop into flame. He takes her hand and studies it: an angry welt from the hot grill. He sees her left eye is swollen too, the flesh around it black and yellow. A few days old.

'Did he do that?'

She nods her head. He looks over his shoulder, but Gordon is in his garage, fussing about in a toolbox. He lifts his head briefly and looks in Frank's direction. The gaze goes right through him.

a mantelpiece photograph

The wind stalls briefly and the mist clears. The river runs. Smoke blooms over the collieries. Plumes of diabolical black rise into the sky. They are fixed for the slimmest moment, stood like statues above the Tyne, atop a wall by waste ground: pools of petrol and tufts of grass. Weeds have gathered in the cracked concrete. A flock of starlings like gunshot is printed on the sky. Wallsend in spring light. A normal Easter Sunday. This is their domain. Their patch, from where Laurence administers justice. It is carved out of brick, the steeply cobbled streets rising behind them. A wrecking ball stands, mid-sweep before a wall. The dust anticipates its sprawl and billows down the road. A fine, thin powder fills the air. Brick dust, cement, asbestos. Laurence stands proud, looking down river. Suited and booted. Each massive crane stands firm: the last of their kind, their enormous heads dipped to the river. Soon there'll be nothing here but shopping centres, they say. But no one is listening. Frank stands beside his mother looking east. Gordon west, like they're looking at the different ends of a single tragedy. Look at their clobber. The tics pinched at the throat, Laurence's perfect knot, the svelte jackets and well-pressed cords. Brylcreem. Partings. Gran in her chiffon blouse. Lilac. Same as her hair. Bright-eyed. Her irises green as acorns. Carol with her sugar-sculpted quiff, shocking purple. The metal in her face glimmers like sweat, like dew. In her right hand she has a hold of Gordon's and in her left, her fingers are entwined in Frank's. The still moment before violence. Anything could happen. The whole tableau might shatter in an instant. Beyond, the ships are gripped in their histories, welded in place. The river is so blue it is ridiculous. The clouds so white. For a moment it all seems real. The colours move through sepia and black and white into Ektachrome. The way the light moves, even in stillness. How it sweeps up the Tyne. There are no words for it. Everything is played out, and yet, nothing is played out.

wallsend - newcastle 1978

Frank watches his father walk among the tables of the working men's club: magisterial, commanding, hands raised in welcome or salute, a heartfelt shake of camaraderie or a slap on the back. King in his own kingdom. Sunday lunchtime and the club is heaving. Their table is piled with empties: Federation, Double Maxim, whisky chasers. The stripper is down to her bra and knickers. She holds a tennis racket and is hitting imaginary balls around the hall. The lads down front are baying for *tits oot*, but she hangs on grimly, bending over and shaking her arse at them.

'Morons,' says Frank.

'Beats Billie Jean King,' says Gordon, and he winks at Carol, who shakes her head at him.

Laurence comes over, a wide tray brimming with drinks, peanuts and cheese rolls. He grins at them and puts a pint down in front of each of his sons, a Bacardi and coke for Carol.

'Gran'll kill me, getting the baps in. Slaving over the roast all day.'

He laughs as he takes a stool and lights an Embassy.

His grey hair is freshly washed and falls to the collar. As always on a Sunday his chops are cleanly shaven. Immaculate in suit and tie, his bright eyes piercing the gloom. He looks at Gordon, as if he were studying a pockmarked sculpture.

'Watch the fucking stripper,' says Gordon.

'Don't be daft, lad.'

'Well stop gawping at me.'

Laurence takes a bite of his bap and chews and watches him. 'How did the job go?' he asks.

'Piece of piss,' says Gordon.

Laurence casts a glance at Frank and Frank squirms. His father shakes his head.

'What happened?'

'Nowt happened,' says Gordon.

Laurence looks across at Carol.

'Were you there, lass?'

'I was in the car,' she says.

'I should have put you in charge,' he says. He nods towards Gordon. 'This pillock is a liability.'

'It's none of my business, Laurence,' she says.

'More's the pity. You'd make a better mobster than mummy's boy, here. I don't know what you see in him.'

He takes a drink, half a pint in one go. 'I had a call from the Super this morning,' he says, turning finally to Frank. 'Some corpse was washed off a slag heap up near Ashington late last night and ended up in the river. Minus a fucking head. The last thing I need right now, or any fucking time, is bother from the coppers. Well?'

Laurence looks at each of them then shakes his head and turns away towards the window. Frank follows his father's gaze. Against the gathering dark, the blue star of the brewery glows. It swings in the wind like a beacon calling the lost and lonely. Scottish & Newcastle, 1978: the land of plenty. A gust of rain batters the cut glass. Rivers run down the panes. His father drinks deeply of his brown ale.

Jackie, Eddie's son, walks past and waves at them.

'You alright, son?' asks Laurence.

'I'm looking for me pa,' he says.

'You shouldn't be in here, lad. This is no place for kids.'

The boy shrugs and turns and wanders down the line of tables. When he's gone, Gordon sniggers.

'What you laughing at?' asks Laurence.

'We know it was Eddie in the sack.'

His father rises off his seat and slaps the boy across the face. Gordon recoils and touches his cheek.

'It split open. That's all,' Gordon continues.

'You think it's a joke? That we do these things for a laugh?' says Laurence.

'What things?'

'You have no idea. Things that can bring a man to his knees.' He looks at Carol and her calm, implacable face seems to calm him a little. 'These things aren't easy.'

Frank drinks his Fed in silence. Why can he never stand up for Gordon? He's just as culpable. More so. But as usual he feels afraid to intervene. He watches Carol, her face full of sympathy for Gordon. How she hates it when Laurence picks on him. He hates how cowardly he himself looks too, how ineffectual. She casts him a quick glance, as if in confirmation, and Frank looks away. His father taps another Embassy on the tabletop and lights up. Laurence turns towards him and blows smoke over his head. All he ever sees in his father's eyes is disappointment.

'What happened then, with Eddie?' asks Gordon.

'You don't need to know, son.'

'We just do the dirty work?' says Frank.

'One day you can be the widow-maker, Frank,' he says. 'See how that feels.'

'He was one of us,' says Frank. It's not right.'

'Grow up, son. It's a code of honour. Any idea what that means? You do the wrong thing and you pay the price.'

Frank sees the bashed-in face laid against the coal slag. It seems incredible. He catches his father's downward glance and realises he's been wringing his hands. Laurence turns away with a look of disgust.

'A long, long time ago,' says Laurence, 'King Henry himself got pissed off with the archbishop. The Pope's own man. Sent two lads. We're talking medieval now, when Heaven and Earth were black and white. Walked into Canterbury Cathedral, without a care, and chopped the fucker's head off. How does that happen?'

'What you on about?' says Frank.

Laurence pours the last of the brown ale into his glass. The bubbles rise close to the rim, then settle. He takes a drink and wipes his mouth.

'When you know you're going to Hell. When God

almighty himself is watching and is going to sit in judgement, you still walk up the fucking aisle and nobble the cunt? If I had an army of men like that I'd own this fucking place.'

'You already do,' says Gordon.

'Loyalty and sacrifice.' It comes out of Laurence's mouth like a hiss. 'Something you two wouldn't have a clue about.'

He turns away from them, tapping his foot to the jukebox. Roy Orbison: 'Only the Lonely'. Frank counts the bottles on the tabletop. His father has finished five pints, and several Bell's already. How does he do it? He's not even drunk.

'You coming over for Sunday dinner, Carol?' Laurence wonders. 'Gran would by delighted to see you.'

'I've got me mam cooking, Laurence. Can I take Gordon back to mine for dinner? We got family round today.'

Frank knows this is untrue. She's being chivalrous, protecting Gordon from any more humiliation. He feels a stab of jealousy.

'Be my bloody guest, lass.'

Frank watches Laurence rise and walk across the room. A man of stature. Respected. Everyone stopping to chat. To pass the time of day. His loud laugh echoes across the room. A man among men. He knows his father has high hopes for him: *Frank Bridge. King of Northumberland. All of this will be yours.* But he realises he's nothing like his father. He has none of the certainties that Laurence has. He's not even sure he cares. Frank fingers the change in his trouser pocket, works the coins like a worry-charm. He'd rather be somewhere else, away from this place. Frank thinks of his gran back at the house, slaving away in the kitchen. How she turns up each Sunday morning to cook the roast, even though she hates the guts of her son-in-law. She does it for love. She does it for Frank and Gordon. He can't wait to get back home and help her.

—

After tea, Frank finds his brother up to his neck in grease and grime, fixing the engine on Laurence's car. He's bent over, working bolts and cutting wires, absorbed, happy now to be under the bonnet. He lifts some large metal structure from the dark mouth of the Wolseley and inspects it. Frank goes over, leans on the other wing and stares in.

'What's that, Gogs?'

'That is what you call a fucked dynamo.' Gordon sniggers at something Frank has no inkling of.

'What's it do?'

'It does the electrics. You know, like the dynamo on a bike, and it feeds the battery too. If this is fucked then the car just conks out, eventually.'

He places it, carefully, in a cardboard box beside the car. 'Died on him yesterday, rush hour, smack in the middle of Newcastle. Left him high and dry outside Woolworths.' He sniggers again, more fitfully this time and shakes his head. 'Hadn't a fucking clue where to go, what bus. No cash on the cunt. If Carol hadn't been driving by he'd still be fucking there.'

He laughs out loud now, tears rolling down his face. He wipes them with the back of his hand. Frank laughs too at the thought of their father lost on the high street.

'Fucking Wolseley. Wouldn't be seen dead in one of these.'

'You still after a Capri, Gogs?'

'Never afford that, will I? Not on the piss he pays me.'

'I'll help, Gogs. I can loan the cash. Some of it.'

His brother shrugs.

'Fucking Woolworths,' he sniggers again.

When Laurence emerges with a mug of tea, their mirth subsides. Their father watches from the kitchen step. Frank can see the suspicion in his gaze, dubious as to the wisdom of letting Gordon work on his car, but he's too tight to pay a mechanic when he can get it for free.

'What you putting in there?' he wants to know.

'An alternator. More efficient than a dynamo. A bit of a fiddle, but nowt I can't bodge.'

He laughs from under the bonnet.

'Bodge that and I'll fucking brain you.'

'Yes, sir!' he says, a tone of sarcasm in his voice.

Laurence puts down his mug of tea, picks up a spanner and walks over to Gordon with a look of menace on his face.

'Talk to me like that and I'll fucking clobber you, lad.'

He waves the spanner in Gordon's face. 'Now stop pissing about and get it fixed,' he says. 'And when it's fixed, I want it washed and polished.'

Laurence turns and goes back inside with his tea. Frank once again wonders at the pleasure it gives his father to make Gordon feel so small. Excruciating to witness, the look of helplessness in Gordon's eyes. The humiliation.

'You OK, Gogs?'

'Next time I'll wire a fucking bomb in.'

When the job's done, he cleans the spark plugs with a cloth and checks the oil. He pulls a long, thin rod of metal out of the engine, like something a matador might do, and studies the blue depth of oil on its tip.

'What's that?' asks Frank.

'That's a fucking dipstick, ya nob,' and they crack up laughing.

cáceres 1988

It's almost noon when Frank wakes a little hungover and wanders into the kitchen, where Lucía is breaking eggs into a bowl. Potato slices sizzle in a frying pan. Tortilla de patatas.

'Cariño. ¿Cómo dormiste?'

'Like a log', he says, yawning. 'Necesito café.'

He pours a strong black coffee from the percolator into a glass, sugars and stirs. He smells it, swirls it and takes a hit. He rinses his glass under the tap and goes to stand behind her, arms around her waist, watching her cook: a shake of the pan, the swirling of eggs, a scattering of paprika, pungent and smoky. The kitchen fills with its scent. The diamond in her wedding ring shimmers against the black stovetop. It fills him with joy. Why did he take so long? He's surprised she waited for him. The tortilla takes a while to set. He lets his hands settle on her stomach. Was that a kick he felt? When she comes to the flip, he stands back to give her space. This is the bit he dreads. When the bottom half is done, she slips a plate over the top and turns the whole thing upside down, then off the plate it slides, with a hiss, back into the frying pan.

'How do you do that?'

'Es fácil,' she says. 'And now, we wait.'

They hold each other, close and slow, accompanied by the subtle sounds of the kitchen: the gurgles and hisses, the hum of the fridge, the coffee pot bubbling. How easy it is to find happiness, he thinks. The tortilla when it's done is perfectly moist in the middle. Best with bread, butter and a café con leche. They spend an hour by the pool. Lucía marks her papers, her undergrad and MA dissertations. She tells him how glad she is to have these holidays, to escape the stress of academic life, to get out of Barcelona for the Easter break and find her soul again. Frank agrees. He loves these days together. He works on a new story. It's a struggle. He's hopeless at plot, but he's learning all the time. He's had a few successes in literary magazines, but nothing spectacular. A notebook full of derivative, Lorca-esque poems, which he knows will never get published. He watches her work. How centred she seems. He feels a fraud at times, living off her the way he does: the villa in both their names, a joint bank account. Her generosity is beyond his comprehension. He contributes nothing. She tells him he should just write, become a novelist, that she will be his benefactor. Like D. H. Lawrence and Lady Ottoline Morrell. It's an image that makes them both laugh. She tells him how disappointed she is with her students. How they lack originality. All the same tropes, the same arguments, the same research sources. He should go to university, she tells him, that he has the aptitude, the brain, the sensitivity, but he just shrugs. No one from Wallsend ever goes to university. He reads the paper, shipped from England, a few days old. It's the best you can do, but it keeps him up to date with the football.

She drops him off in the village and he kisses her through the open window. A smile between them. He's blessed. He sits at the local bar sipping a cold fino, smoking cigarettes in the sun. It's hot for the time of year. He notices a car. British plates. A man with a hat gets out and goes into the tobacconist. He looks at Frank, but Frank pays him no notice.

It's a long walk home, but one he enjoys, having bought bread and vegetables, cheese, chorizo and a bottle of Rioja; a nice late lunch on the patio. The pueblo is scented with citrus blossom, almond and olive. As far as he can see, an ocean of white flowers blows in the groves; sweet, intoxicating. Spain this time of year never fails to seduce. It's when the country wakes up from its short, winter slumbers: the festivals, the parties, fiesta time when the streets are pungent and life seems endlessly abundant. He turns off the road and heads up the track to the house. He notices the tyre tracks in the dust. Deep and wide and well defined. An expensive car. He thinks about the one he'd seen earlier, the man with the hat, and it all comes rushing in. He feels nauseous, breathless. He drops his bags in the dust and gets down on his haunches. He can hardly breathe. When he stands, he looks around him. He scans the distance for signs. Nothing moves in the vast landscape, but he senses a great storm has passed this way and left in its wake an absence of everything.

sierra de cádiz 2003

Frank wanders with his coffee onto the patio. Gordon is working in his garage. Some beast of a car. God knows what it is. It looks like something out of the movies, big and brash, but pretty knocked-up. The windows are cracked and sit awkwardly in the doors and the bodywork is rusted in places. The bonnet is up and Gordon is working on the engine. The car port has a pleasing smell of oil and petrol and polish, a touch of rubber at the back of the nose. He watches his brother for a while. His concentration is total. He doesn't notice Frank watching him.

'Gogs.'

'Jesus,' he says, turning to his brother. 'What you up to?'

'What kind of car is this?'

Gordon straightens up and stretches his back.

'It's a Mustang Boss 1971. Turned up in Algeciras, some scrap dealer. Worth a fortune, this beauty. Or will be when I've done with it.' He stretches his back, his arms, eases a shoulder, then looks at Frank, pondering. 'I don't suppose the bastard left me owt.'

'It all went to me, Gogs.'

'Course it did. What a bastard.'

'You did completely fuck him over and disappear with a van full of loot, Gogs.'

'I could contest.'

'You could. But not from here. You'd have to get home for that.'

Gordon studies him a moment and Frank sees his eyes narrow

'You're pissing with me.'

'I'm only guessing.'

'I'm not going back, Frank.'

'That's up to you, mate. I only came here to tell you that Dad had died. Nowt else.'

'Out of the goodness of your heart.'

'If you like.'

'I don't know what you're up to.'

'I could give you half.'

'And why would you do that?'

'Why not?'

'I doubt it.'

'When I was there, in the nursing home, he was talking about you coming home. "Gordon is coming home," he kept on saying. I didn't know what the hell he was talking about. "Gordon is coming home, Frank is bringing him." You know. I was sitting right there and he's telling me all this shit.'

'A basket case by the sounds of it,' he says, and laughs.

'It wasn't funny. It was painful, seeing him like that.'

'My heart bleeds.'

'You never thought of going back? Even for a bit? You must miss the place.'

'And the welcome party, waiting on the quayside, eh? That psycho Welby and his henchmen?'

'I've told you, Gogs. Believe me. There is no gang. Those days are over.'

'Forget it, Frank.' He puts his head back beneath the bonnet. 'Trouble with these old Yankie cars is getting the parts. You need to think creatively, find a workaround. Otherwise you have to source stuff from the States. It takes forever. I can't be fucked with that.'

Frank turns away from him and wanders out. He's surprised by how sad he feels for his brother. He seems lost. All at sea. Maybe he will split the inheritance. He feels a need to talk. To get everything off his chest. Not just about their father, but about all of them. The past, the future, if there is one. He wants to talk to Gordon, to tell him how things have changed back home, how he wouldn't recognise the place these days: the Millennium Bridge, the Baltic. The Metro. How St James' Park would blow his mind if he could see it. He wants to unburden himself too, he can't deny it, but Gordon could never be his father confessor. Gordon doesn't care, one way or the other.

He sits for a while in a deckchair beside the pool. He feels maudlin. Homesick for once. He thinks about his last visit with Laurence. Just before he died. That glum, depressing place, full of wasted lives. He'd talked about his sons. How good they were. How they would soon be reconciled. He looked ruined. Desiccated. If you touched him, he would turn to dust. When he'd done with his father and left the nursing home, he'd walked down to the docks to look at the old place. The Tyne was not what it used to be. He hardly recognised the banks it flowed between. All the change, the Neptune Yard had disappeared, the naval docks at Walker likewise; only the great Swan Hunter remained. But its time was marked. Gone the great days of the *Mauretania*, the *Ark Royal*. The railway gone: the riverside branch. The pits. The steelworks. Suddenly a great silence. This was never a quiet place. Such silence would have driven his grandfather mad. All he knew was the screech of girder on girder, the tearing of metal things, huge mechanical wheels turning, heaving chains, rivet guns pounding bolts into steel, the echo bouncing from one side of the river to the other. The wails of ships. The horns that shook the bedrooms of Wallsend. You could feel them in the mattress as you slept. Now there was just the distant hum of traffic on its way to Whitley Bay and the dead lands beyond. The pubs were gone, the long since derelict Ship, where he'd courted Carol. On the far bank, nothing. Jarrow, that once great behemoth of industrial England, stood mute. He'd watched a couple pull their car up against the river and fall out. He could hear their laughter. They smoked in the river light, two strangers. One of them flicked a butt in the Tyne. Just students. They got back in the car and drove away.

It wasn't all bad. The town itself was thriving; there

was money, infrastructure, regeneration, a vision of sorts, but down here, he looked towards his father's holdings, his warehouses and keeps: all gone. All that was left of his father's empire, such as it was, cash and carries now and IKEA. Frank had laughed. At what he wasn't sure. This was not the Alhambra, the Mezquita de Sevilla, those great legacies of the Moors. No. This was Tyneside and he'd felt a great regret. A deep sense of loss.

cáceres 1988

As he nears the villa he takes a detour through an olive grove. He crouches and scans. There's no one there. He skirts the villa and puts his bag against the back wall. He sees the car, the one he'd seen earlier, parked out of view. He kneels in the shade, heart pounding. Lucía is innocent. They must know that. She'll be fine, he tells himself, though he knows it's a lie. The last few ribbons of heat shimmer in the stifling air. How did they find him? He curses himself. He's been careless. He's put her in great jeopardy.

He'll have to wait until dark. He can't think of another option, and even then, what will he do? He waits in the shadows. Dusk comes quickly at this latitude, a brief and breathtaking blush in the western sky, the sun red as a cherry tomato, the brilliant pinprick of Venus and suddenly, it's dark.

He gathers the courage to make a move. He goes towards their car. The keys are still in the ignition. He opens the door, reaches in and takes them. He locks it and puts the keys in his pocket. He runs at a half crouch towards the house. He can hear them talking through the open kitchen window. He stands back at a safe distance, to get a better look. The sweet advantage of being outside, in the dark. They can see nothing but their own reflections in the glass, whereas he can see everything. It's lit like a stage. Two guys. He recognises them from home. One is Macca, which is good. The other is Welby, which is less good. One idiot and one psychopath. They've been at the drinks cabinet and the table is already littered with empty bottles: a litre of whisky, two thirds done. A bottle of gin, beers. That's one thing in Frank's favour. He crouches and makes his way to the wall beside the kitchen door, as close to them as he dares. He leans and takes a look. She's laid on the floor. Face down. A blackened hole in the side of her head. He turns away, his stomach heaving. He runs back to the rear of the villa. He pukes as he runs. He can't keep it down. It erupts against the fence. Tears come hot and fierce. A savage heat burns in his core. In his soul. He needs to scream. This is the end of everything. He punches the ground, the hard dusty ground, and feels his knuckles crack. He's on his haunches again. Head in hands. Not this. He has to pull himself together. He breathes, at last. Compose yourself. Blank it. He takes deep breaths. He goes back to the window. He won't look there. He studies the men. The men who have killed his wife. The two men who are going to die tonight.

He waits. Soon enough Welby lays his gun on the kitchen table and wanders out.

'I need a piss,' he says, 'stop here.'

Frank stares at the gun. It glimmers, a jet-black artefact, the smooth and elegant silencer mouthing a silent O on the tabletop. He knows what happens next. It's written somewhere. Was it a dream? The other man, Macca, is agitated, nervous. Why the hell did they send Macca? He doesn't know what to do with himself, then he too wanders out of the kitchen, down the hall and onto the patio and Frank, without hesitation opens the kitchen door. Its hinges scream in the silent night. He gets the gun and slips back out under cover of darkness. He's wide awake. Ready. The odds have flipped in his favour. It's a miracle. They wander back into the kitchen and pour more drinks. Welby reaches for the gun. It's not there. He looks around the room.

'You got my gun?'

'No, mate.'

'Where's my fucking gun?'

Frank can hear the panic in his voice. It sounds good.

'He's here. The fucker's here. How's he got in?' shouts Welby. He sweeps the bottles and glasses off the kitchen table with a shattering that rings through the house.

'Get the twelve bore.'

'He might be out there, Wells.'

Welby shoves him against the table.

'Get the fucking twelve bore.'

Macca shoves back at him, petulant, then turns and goes to the car.

A dog barks in the distance. Another dog answers back. Frank watches Welby now, alone in the kitchen. He can sense the panic, the awful fear of having lost the edge. Frank steps inside.

'Hello, Welby.'

Welby stares at him, incredulous. He looks at the pistol and Frank shoots him in the face. Welby drops, and slumps against the fridge, muttering something. Frank puts in another one, dead centre of his chest, and Welby goes still. He doesn't dare turn to look at Lucía. Not yet.

'Fucking car's locked,' shouts Macca as he steps back in the villa. He comes into the kitchen and sees Frank with the gun pointing at him. He puts his hands up.

'Put 'em down Macca, it's not a fucking Western.'

Macca looks at Welby, dead against the fridge. He registers no emotion. Frank gestures his gun down towards the body of Lucía.

'It wasn't me, Frank.'

'I should put a bullet in your head.'

'It wasn't.'

'I know it wasn't,' he shouts, loudly, and Macca flinches. Frank shakes his head. 'Fuck this, Macca. Just fucking fuck this.'

'You gonna kill me, Frank?'

'I'd like to. Believe me. What was the plan here, tell me? Did they send you to kill us?'

'No, Frank, just to get you back home, that's all.'

'Another fuck-up.'

Macca shrugs.

'What the fuck. And Lucía. Jesus. What the holy fuck?'

'I dunno. Welby just went mad when you weren't here. Lost his rag. You know what he's like.'

His head is a mess. He feels on the edge of mayhem, a terrible seething inside him. The urge to do damage, but Macca is no use to him dead. If both men fail to return home, they'll just send more. Frank is going to have to let him go back. Trust him. Of all the lads, Macca is just about the only one he can trust. The only one stupid enough.

'Macca?'

Macca's bottom lip quivers.

'What, Frank.'

'Go back home. Tell Laurence it went tits up. He won't have any problem believing that. Tell him everyone died. You got that, Macca.'

'Yes, Frank.'

'And you get to live. But Macca—'

'What?'

'If anything happens, I will hunt you down and I will slaughter you, and then I will come after your family and murder every one of them. Slowly. Do you understand?'

'Thank you.'

'Fucking thank you. Jesus. Do you understand?'

'Yes.'

He walks out to the patio, and Macca follows him. The mesa, immense and dark, stretches out beyond them, a half-moon drifting through wisps of cumulus. He can hear something moan out there, an animal, or is it just the wind? Dead now, to everything, numb to the majesty of this monumental land. He's a man alone in a world vast and terrifying.

He turns back to Macca.

'Macca.'

'What?'

He needs to explain, to tell Macca how deep the darkness is. To explain how it feels.

'Nothing.'

He walks out to Lucía's car and opens the door.

'Take this. It'll be safer. Drive north, to Bilbao, ditch the motor, and get the ferry back to Plymouth. You got your passport, Macca?'

'Yes.'

'Christ, I don't believe it. You got money?'

'Welby has it.'

They go back inside the villa. Frank opens Welby's coat. It's drenched in blood. He gets the wallet from the inside pocket. A tonne of cash, pesetas and pounds. He hands it to Macca.

'OK, Macca. Just keep driving until you reach the port. Don't stop, and don't fuck about.'

When Macca has gone, the silence is absolute. He looks at her, at last. He can't bear it. He wants to see her face, to kiss it, but he can't, he's scared of what he will see. Everything gone, in an instant. How the hell is he going to fix all this? Tonight, he will go mad. He will burn the house down. He will disappear.

He picks up the gun and carries it out to the septic tank. He lifts the metal grate, and the rank stink of it hits him at the back of the nose. He drops the gun into the sump and closes it away. Forever. This is the end of violence, he thinks. Two bodies. He carries one outside and lays it carefully on the parched earth, under the lemon tree. He can't even consecrate it. He doesn't know how. He covers it with a sheet. The other he leaves, slumped against the fridge. He has to go. He sits on the patio in the warm night air and drinks. He feels like a drowning man, surfacing momentarily, then sinking again. He wants to sink forever. He drops the bottle on the stone floor with a smash. An end to that also. Will he survive? He doesn't think so. He'll try.

From the outhouse, he grabs the spare petrol. He goes back to the villa and drenches the furniture. He drenches the beds upstairs and finally the hallway as he heads outside. He takes a last look at the place. He feels empty. All it takes is a single match. He gets into Welby's car and drives. A few hours ago, he was walking home for lunch with his wife. Now, she and their unborn child are dead. He has murdered a man in cold blood. And like Lot, he is fleeing the maelstrom. It glows in his wing mirror, ferocious red-and-yellow flame as he drives down the track towards the motorway and the Portuguese border.

sierra de cádiz 2003

He walks behind the villa to Carol's allotment. An oasis in a parched landscape. Verdant and fecund. The greenery gives off a welcoming cool. It rises from the dark spaces under the broad leaves, the damp, mulched earth where someone has watered recently. He finds huge, pendulous courgettes, yellow and green. Insects buzz in their gaping flowers. Tomatoes, every shape and size. Aubergines, plump almost to bursting. Artichokes five foot high, shaking their spiky fists at the sky. Against a fence a dense tangle of strawberries grows: raspberries, blueberries. Plum trees. Oranges.

Here she comes, up the path, like Eve in the first garden. A new pair of sunglasses covering her eyes, a sheepish grin on her face. He takes her glasses off and looks at her.

'How long has this been going on?'

She touches her bruised cheek.

'That's how it is, Frank.'

'He's crazy.'

'He thinks the world's against him.'

'What's he got to worry about? He's living in paradise and doesn't even know it. Look at this place.'

'He's like a child.'

'What does he do all day?'

'Plays with his cars. Does them up and sells them on, mainly to dealers in the UK, sometimes America. It's the only thing he cares about.'

She turns away, deadheads a few roses with a snap of her fingers. She looks back towards the house, as if checking that Gordon is not there.

'You can't live like this, Carol.'

'Call me Caz,' she says, 'you never called me Carol before.'

He reaches out and takes her hand.

'I hate it. I'm just—.' She breaks off for a moment and looks across the mountains. 'It's so difficult,' she continues. 'I mean, I love the place. The weather. Look at this garden. I could never have this back home. Imagine this in Newcastle?'

'Cabbages and tatties maybe.'

Carol laughs and puts her arms around him. It's a hesitant, half-hearted hug. He can feel the awkward gravity between them. He breathes in that perfume again.

'Was it Dawn gave you the address?'

Frank nods.

'She said there'd been a row. Her and Gordon. That she'd been exiled or something.'

'They hate each other. Last time she visited, she could see what was happening and she wasn't going to let it lie. She told him what she thought of him, and he kicked her out. I miss her so much. She was my last connection with things back home.'

'I'm surprised you didn't leave long ago.'

'I thought about it, but it scares me. I wouldn't last five minutes.'

'There's no one left any more. It's 2003, not 1973.'

'I know you say that, but memories are long up there. They don't forget. There'll be somebody, in some shadowed corner, waiting to settle scores. I know they've been looking for us. I don't want to live like that, scared of every stranger. Continually looking over my shoulder.'

It seems then as if she might cry, but she doesn't. She's too proud for tears. Ex-bride of the docks. One of their own. She shakes her head. 'I love this place.' She gestures around herself. 'I mean, look at it. How could I go back? All that grey, all that cold. What would I do? Get a job in Woollies?

They walk through the gardens. At the far end by a wooden gate, they come to a pomegranate tree. Its heavy globes glow in the last of the sun.

'Oh, look at these,' says Frank.

'Aren't they beautiful?'

It seems unnatural, the way the fruit grows, so plump and heavy on the end of such thin, spindly branches. He goes up to the tree and gazes into its heart. It's like a chandelier. He holds one of the fruits in his palm and squeezes it gently, then twists it off. He holds it out before her.

'You know what it's called in Spanish?'

'No.'

'Granada.'

'Like the town, you mean?'

'Yes. Lorca's town.'

He takes the fruit over to the wooden gate and brings it down hard on the fence post. It splits down the middle and spills its rubies over the back of his hand. He licks them off.

'Let my aching heart break open, like a pomegranate.'

'Is that your poet?'

'It is, yes. Here.'

He gives her the pomegranate and he watches her suck the juice and crunch the pips.

'There's a painting by Rossetti. It's in the Tate, I think. Proserpine eating a pomegranate. God, it's erotic. But sad too. Heartbreaking.'

'Why is it?'

'It's the passing of time, isn't it? Knowledge too, I guess. All that bollocks. Loss of innocence. We all know how that ends.'

'Does she die?'

'Everyone dies,' he says.

'I know, but . . .'

He watches her eat. The inside of the pomegranate really is blood red. Her mouth is wet.

'It's been a long time, Frankie.'

He moves towards her, then stops himself. 'Is there somewhere we can walk?'

'We can go to the gorge,' she says. 'It's not far.'

They walk up the path through ancient olive groves

where his legs brush against marjoram, straggling clumps of wild fennel. He runs his fingers through the fronds and smells their perfume. The air is thick with it. The evening rich with scent.

'What is it about this poet?' she asks, as they climb the gully.

He thinks back to the afternoon in his gran's garden when he first heard the poetry of Federico García Lorca. Lucía reading dreamily, drunkenly his poetry. He tells her about the party, the guitar, the sound of flamenco. He describes the look in Lucía's eyes, how smitten he was by her, and by the strange sounds of the poetry in her mouth. How after Gordon and Carol absconded, the blame settled on him. He was all but run out of town. So he followed her to London and then to Spain and fell in love with her. Married her.

'And where is she, this Lucía?'

He doesn't answer this and turns from her. They stop on the path.

'Well?' she asks.

He looks around himself, gathering words, meaning, where there is none.

'She died a long time ago. It doesn't matter now,' he says, finally.

They stand in the brute sun. The urge to reach out and hold her, to touch her, is like a deep ache in his bones. She's curious. She wants to know more.

'It was a dark time, Caz. I got depressed. I was raging. Drinking like hell. I burned down our villa. Lost everything. I dunno. I couldn't forgive myself. I went awol. Disappeared. That's why everyone thought I was dead. But I headed back to England, eventually. Went to university. Got a degree.'

She takes his hand.

'University? Frank Bridge?'

He laughs when he sees the look on her face.

'I know. It takes some believing. Some old tosser from Wallsend studying Spanish literature. But I really took to it. I guess it kept me in touch with her. Her culture. I loved it. And now, I'm trying to turn things round. Get back on an even keel. Working on this book now. God knows if anyone will take it. But I need to write it. I promised her. I promised myself.'

'You always were the thoughtful one. It's odd how we all ended up here, one way or another.'

'Back then, it would have seemed impossible.'

'I'd have loved to have gone to university.'

'Do it. There's nothing special about it these days.'

Her hand tightens around his fingers. She still lives in the old world, he thinks. This place is like a time capsule, stuck in the seventies. The Pistols. The Vibrators. 'Working Class Hero', all that stuff.

'What would you study?' he wonders.

'English maybe, or art. I used to love painting at school, I was good at it. Poetry. I write poems sometimes. No one ever sees them. There's no one to show them to.'

'I'd love to see them, Caz.'

'No, it's just fun. I do it for therapy. For healing.'

'It's good medicine.'

'Something to do with gardening would be good,' she says. 'Something more practical.'

'Horticulture, maybe. Looks like you already know a load of stuff.'

'It's taken years, a lot of trial and error. A lot of reading too. I reckon I could grow just about anything now. You learn so much from gardening, and not just about gardening. About life.'

'Like how?' he asks.

'About sickness and health, about weakness and withering, you know, the cycle of life, the struggle to survive. It's about nurturing.'

'I never thought of it like that.'

'I'd love to get some bees to help out, but Gordon won't let me.'

'What's his problem?'

'I think he's scared of them,' she laughs.

When they get to the gorge, the view stretches down the coast. In the distance Cádiz gleams, like it's cut from coral. Gateway to Africa and beyond. He thinks of Columbus sailing from there in the fifteenth century. Setting out into a vast unknown. He can see the coast of Morocco in the distance. The peaks of the Atlas Mountains. He lights two cigarettes and offers one to Carol. They linger a while, smoking in silence. He counts the contrails of planes far above, four of them, heading out over open sea. Canaries. Cuba, Mexico City.

'How long you staying, Frankie?'

She's looking at him the way he remembers from long ago. It tears his heart.

'I don't know,' he says. 'I might get off this evening.'

She turns away and looks towards the distant sea.

'So soon? After all this time?'

'Gordon doesn't like me being here. If I stay much longer things could turn nasty.'

'Things are already nasty, Frank.'

He goes to her and holds her against him, the late light already fading. She takes his hand.

'Can you stay the night?' she asks.

They walk to the edge of the ravine. In the distance, the Costas, the brilliant blue sea, all the lands beyond.

She seems lost in thought. Frank stands behind her, close. It feels good to be hugging her. He looks at the land around them, stony, dry, dotted here and there with prickly pear. He lifts her hand and kisses it. The evening sun is large and the savage heat is melting away. The air has a soft, silken feel against the skin. He can smell honeysuckle from somewhere, lemon, thyme.

wallsend - newcastle 1977

Frank walks down to visit Carol at the Ship where she works the daytime shift. This is the dockers' pub beside the Tyne, and every morning she and the other girls pull a hundred pints and line up bottles of brown, of Mackeson, on tables, along the bars and windowsills, waiting for the lunchtime hooter. The pints glow in the river light, amber gold and black, like beakers in a chemistry lab. In the still moment before the siren there are plates of roast potatoes, sausages, ham-and-cheese sandwiches. You can hear the bubbles pop in every glass. The bar staff speak in hushed tones. It feels like church on a Sunday morning. A floor is swept, a hand pump polished, and then it is mayhem as the workers flock in for their lunch break; the Leazes End on a Saturday afternoon, the match-day buzz; exhilarating. The chat and the song, the fighting, the darts and the dominoes. The smell of sweat, of yeast and barley. These are Frank's people. He's known them since he was a kid. He knows their parents and their grandparents by their first names. Most of his old classmates work at the Dolphin Yard and if it hadn't been for his father, a Scot, an outsider, with crueller, more criminal ideas about how to make a living, he would be there too. They drink like madmen. Incredible how many pints a man can drink in thirty minutes. Some of them never make it back for the afternoon shift; a whole day's pay docked and a reckoning back home. When the hooter goes again, the pub empties in seconds and silence rushes back in to fill the tap room. You can hear the river rush by. God knows how the landlord keeps tabs on all the business. The floor is awash with beer, broken glasses and fag butts. Frank watches Carol take the mop and the bucket and swab the floors clean. He loves to watch her move: tough, big boned, elegant but strong. He's seen her put men flat on their backs for touching her up. A single punch. No one messes with Carol.

When they lock up, at half past two, they wander back up the hill, hand in hand. Carol's brolly flaps in the wind, storm clouds gathering, dark and angry, the rain beating above them on the plastic parasol as they sit on a wall by waste ground. A demolition squad takes down a terrace behind them. A whole street. Houses he's known, and been in. Living rooms, kitchens. He can see the peeling wallpaper. The pencil drawings on the kids' bedroom walls. A fireplace hangs, mid-air, levitating, its grate gaping. Improvements they say. For whom?

'Where's Gordon today. You seeing him?' he asks.

'You tell me. Doesn't he work with you?'

'Not really. Gordon's the driver. It's all he can do. All Dad will trust him to do.'

'There's more to Gordon than that.'

'I know, but Dad doesn't see it.'

'You know all he wants is respect, a bit of affection? He wants to be loved, like everyone else. Is that so difficult?'

'He gets plenty of that from you,' he spits.

'Gordon's a free spirit.'

'That's exactly what Laurence hates. There's nothing worse. A lack of direction, of ambition. I think he thinks Gordon is laughing at him in some way. Taking the piss.'

For a moment the rain abates and she leans into him. A tugboat pulls a tanker downstream. It must be a hundred times the tug's size. Incredible how powerful those small boats are.

'I don't know what you see in him, to be honest,' he says.

'He's not really like you. Like Laurence and all his thugs. That's not who he is. One day we'll get out of here, Gordon and me, and say goodbye to all of this. He doesn't fit in. Neither of us fits in, to be honest.'

Frank wants to tell her how that's the way he feels too. That he's playing a game, his father's game. But now he feels stuck. He feels implicated. He wonders what she means by them getting out of here. What's on her mind? He takes her hand and holds it tight.

'He'd blow a valve if he knew about us.'

'You scared of your little brother, Frankie?'

Frank thinks about that. About how volatile Gordon is. How unpredictable. His outbursts can be frightening. Beating the walls with his bare fists. Taking it out on himself.

'No,' he lies.

The Tyne fattens and spreads below them, slouching through the gap between Wallsend and Jarrow, heading to sea. *Not far now*, thinks Frank, *just round the bend, and away*. He has a picture in his head of some distant place, a more pleasant place, with sunshine. He looks down at the shipyards spread below and listens to the noises bounce off the walls of the terraced houses stacked like dominoes on the slopes of the river. The hammering of riveters plating some foreign tanker, whistles, foghorns. The rattle of chains. The shrieks of metal sheets creaking under pressure tear the afternoon wide open. The blue flash of the arc-welders strobing in shadowed alcoves. He likes the way the sparks bounce off the concrete floors, like ball bearings. He recognises each process by its sound. Its signature. If you live here, you work in the shipyard: riveter, boilermaker, plater. You come home in the evening, or sometimes in the morning, covered in shit: spirals of iron shavings, woodchip, your face black with smoke, the whites of your eyes shining. Or sometimes you come home drunk, at midnight, unable to climb the hazardous stone steps to bed. You sleep all night on the sofa, or the kitchen floor. Or worse, if the door is locked, you sleep in the yard by the shitter.

The dark, colossal sheds hum and shake on the water's edge. The massive bulkhead of a half-done pleasure cruiser towers over the quayside. A mass of crane-metal crawls on each bank as far as he can see: the stout and sturdy gantries, the hammerheads like giant pelicans striding off into spring rain. New cranes taking old cranes down, dismantling them. The Jarrow banks are a mass of smoke. Chimney after chimney right down the coast: mines and steelworks.

She holds the umbrella above them, but the drizzle drifts in curtains, horizontal. He looks at her as she gazes at the river below them. She always makes his heart beat faster. Her perfume drifts in the breeze. He looks at her body, tight in her anorak. She smiles and looks back, presses up against him.

'Grab a handful while you can,' she says.

He kisses her and slips his hand inside her coat. She gives a satisfied groan to tell him it's fine, that it feels good.

'Let's get out of this shithole,' he says.

'What do you mean?'

'Let's just go.'

'To town?'

Frank shakes his head and laughs.

'No, not to sodding town. Somewhere else, like you were saying.'

'Where?'

'I dunno. There must be somewhere,' he says.

'What you talking about?' She laughs and ruffles his hair. 'You asking me to run away with you?'

The chat about Gordon, his dreams of escape, his being a free spirit, has caught him off guard. He feels maudlin now. Sentimental for something just beyond him, out of reach and shining brightly.

'I dunno. It all feels wrong.'

97

'What does, Frankie?'

The rain drums above them on the brolly top. Behind them kids are throwing bricks into a ditch.

'Nothing will ever happen here.'

He suggests the club for a few drinks, but she thinks it too risky, suggests a bus to Whitley Bay and a walk on the beach. They could get a few bottles of brown. To Frank it seems suddenly small minded, an easy option; getting mortal in the afternoon. That yearning again, for something more expansive. Something he can't quite fathom. He looks again at the shipyards. The industry below them. If he looks closely, even he, who had never put a shift in, can see the creeping deprivation. Every month it dwindles a little bit more. He can see the occasional concrete space that once housed a welding shed. An idle berth greening up. The wrecking crew behind him, cleaning out the terraces, fewer and fewer ships. More and more lads on the dole. It's on a knife edge now, still thriving, but like his dad says, everything is moving east: Korea, China, Japan. *You're lucky we're in a safer business, son.* He can see his father's lock-ups, the fortified warehouses full of contraband. Whisky mainly, which he ships abroad. All manner of stuff he's not allowed to see. He's heard talk of currency, marijuana. Maybe the hard stuff. He doesn't know.

His grandad liked to talk about when he was a kid, when the whole river was chock full. You couldn't see the water for fucking ships, he'd say. And the sky was dark as stout. Soot and fumes billowed like fury into the air. The whole of the North East was a ferment of kiln and furnace, smokestack and billowing chimneys. You spent your life coughing your guts out. It was uplifting. Religious.

He puts his arm around Carol's waist and pulls her to him. They wander through the shattered terraces, the wrecked yards and outhouses, over the broken brick walls.

'Look,' she says, and pulls him into a darkened, empty dining room, long since lost to its table and sideboard and family china. It's almost dry and the sound of the machinery has dwindled to a muffled roar. She pulls him to her and kisses his mouth, hard.

'Let's do it.'

'Caz.'

'I want it,' she says.

She lifts her dress and they fumble in the blustery wreck of this ruined home. Somewhere, the kids who'd lived here would be weeping. Their mother would be banging her head against the pristine plaster walls of a new high-rise in Byker. He thinks he recognises the house, the wallpaper, the yellow lino still stuck to the kitchen floor. A slanting rain falls beyond the broken-glass-topped wall, against the rubble in the concrete yard where a rocking horse, its runners and hind legs smashed, looks up at him, stricken and pathetic, its wide eyes full of reproach. Rain has slicked its equine head. He bites her throat and sucks. It's all hands and awkward groping, desperate and indelicate. Fabric is torn. What it is, he can't be sure. She's heavier than he imagines when he tries to lift her, or perhaps he's just too weak. She turns herself around to face the wall. It's easier that way, her palms, both of them, flat against the brickwork. He doesn't hesitate. The diggers work beyond the wall. He imagines them breaking through at last and finding them, desperate and shameful, half in, half out, his trousers round his ankles, his hairy arse going like a jackhammer. Skinny legs grotesque in the gloom. He doesn't know if she comes. As soon as he's finished, he pulls out and slumps against her.

'I'm sorry,' he says.

She wriggles back into her knickers and straightens her dress, clapping the brick dust off her hands. Frank looks at her, sheepish, somewhat appalled, his stomach churning. Carol laughs at the look of him.

'Don't worry, Frankie. We can do it anytime you want to.'

She pushes her arm through his and they wander out into the drizzle and noise. Frank stops by the rocking horse and kicks it in the teeth. Its porcelain head shatters against his toecap. He looks down at the remnants laid in the rubble. What the hell's up with him? Carol stands beneath her umbrella watching with some amusement. He takes a quick glance at her as they make their way to the offie. She seems untroubled by the whole experience, but all is not well with him. Something is shifting inside him and Frank doesn't think he can contain it.

sierra de cádiz 2003

Frank opens the kitchen door and finds Gordon and Carol face to face, smooching to some dreadful James Last. He watches them for a moment. It's like nothing has happened. Carol yelps as Gordon grabs her arse. Has Frank misjudged things? They pull apart when they realise he's there, and Frank notes the sheepish look on Carol's face.

'Don't mind me,' he says.

Gordon laughs and takes a swig of his brandy. It's cooler now, but Frank drips. The physicality of the heat, the way the night holds you in a bear hug.

'Fancy a dance, Frankie?' asks Carol.

She's turning, provocatively, arms moving above her head, fingers curling in a parody of flamenco braceo. He watches her a moment, then takes a look at Gordon topping up his brandy glass.

'No thanks, Caz.'

'Dance with her, Frank. What's the matter with you? Still scared of the ladies?'

'What you on about?'

'You never understood women, Frank. Women aren't interested in brains.'

He grabs at Carol again, but this time she wriggles out of his grasp with a laugh.

'Sit down, Gordon, before you have a heart attack,' she says.

He slumps in his armchair and lights up a fat cigar. 'Big balls, and a good seeing to, Frank. Fucking book worms never pull the birds.'

Carol is studying Frank from the end of her cigarette, an inscrutable look on her face. He wonders if he's changed the atmosphere. He feels the joy flow out of the room, if that's what it was. He can't make anything out. There's a tension as soon as the three of them get together. They watch him from their separate corners. Gordon seems wound up again, suddenly, and Carol too is agitated, confrontational. He clenches his fist. For a moment he wishes he was down in Cádiz, enjoying a fish dinner in the cooling sea breezes, far away from all this crap.

'You gonna tell us some poems, Frankie,' Carol asks, finally, breaking the silence.

'Not tonight.'

'Come on, Frankie, give us a poem,' she says.

She knows how volatile Gordon can be, but now she's poking and probing, as if she's no idea what will rile him. Or maybe she does. Frank looks over at Gordon, who empties his glass.

'Gogs isn't interested in poetry, Caz,' says Frank.

'Fuck Gogs, I wanna hear one.'

She's drunk. She's goading him. Goading them both. It's a dangerous game.

'Put some fucking Elvis on,' says Gordon.

'Please Frankie,' she says.

She pulls the cork out of her sherry bottle and tops herself up.

'For fuck's sake, just read one,' says Gordon. 'Put the cunt out of her misery.'

Frank looks at him sat in his armchair. Despot in a foreign land. His eyes have a look of menace about them. He's halfway down a bottle of Martell and his face shines with sweat, his double chin. This damned weather. Half nine at night and it's touching the 30s. He's parched. He pours a glass of water and drinks. *Fuck them both*, he thinks, *get it over and done with*. He closes his eyes and speaks the words he knows by heart. The words his beautiful wife taught him, a long time ago.

'No quiero que me repitan que los muertos no pierden la sangre,' he says, then pauses. What comes next, he wonders. His mind goes blank.

'Hang on.'

They stand in silence, gawping.

'Que la boca podrida sigue pidiendo agua,' he says, at last, raising his glass of water.

Gordon is aghast.

'You speak the lingo?'

'It's not that hard, Gogs. Anyone could learn it.'

'What's it mean?' she asks.

'Who fucking cares?' says Gordon.

'Let's drop it, Caz.'

'No. Tell me.'

Frank takes a tea towel off the countertop and wipes his forehead.

'Something like: don't keep telling me the dead don't bleed, that the rotting mouth still begs for water.'

'That's deep,' says Carol.

'Deep as my arse hole.'

'Fuck off, Gordon,' says Carol.

They sit for a while, exhausted. The heat is oppressive, physical. Too hot to think. Frank feels the sweat roll down his spine as the kitchen falls into silence.

'They were violent times,' says Frank, eventually. 'The fascists were killing everyone. They shot him in 1936. Assassinated at the side of a road. Not far from here.'

'Why? What did he do?'

'Nothing. He was just a poet. And a homosexual. It's said they shot him up the arse.'

Gordon laughs.

'I thought that might appeal to you. Spain's greatest poet. Who'd want to murder a poet?'

Gordon snorts.

'You'll never change, Gogs.'

'Why should I?'

'The world has changed, that's why. Though you wouldn't know it, living up here.'

'You've had a bump on the head, mate.'

'Let's change the subject,' says Frank.

'You always did think you were better than everyone else.'

Frank studies the face of his brother, a picture of

bitterness. He takes a stool at the breakfast bar and wonders what the nights must be like here, these two combustibles mixing it up in the stifling heat. Dancing one moment, kicking chunks out of each other the next. It must be terrifying. Or maybe not, maybe it's him, Frank, who's the catalyst for all this tension.

'Just go to bed, Gordon, you're a waste of space,' says Carol.

'Fuck you.'

Carol groans. She looks over at Frank. Her eyes are blurred. She's been drinking most of the day.

'It threatens him, Frank. Poetry.' She looks back at Gordon. 'Doesn't it, love? All that romance, all that emotion.'

She walks over to his chair and stands over him.

'Your big bull heart can't take it. So full of hate and jealousy.'

He bows his head and spits on the floor. When he looks up at her, she slaps him across the face.

Gordon knocks his brandy glass off the arm of the chair and rises. For a moment he's speechless. He stands before her, shaking. Frank sees how his fists clench, the way they always have.

She looks over to Frank.

'I should have stayed with you, Frankie. We had a good thing going, back in the day. I threw it all away. For this slob.'

Her words hang in the still, night air. Frank winces. A pulse throbs in his temple.

Gordon looks at him briefly, then turns away as if he hasn't heard and he stumbles towards her, his great, fat hand raised above her head. He hits her with the full, pink meat of it and she drops. Frank leaps off his stool and grabs him by the arm, pulling him off balance. They stagger around the kitchen together. Gordon panting, breathless. He struggles in Frank's grip, trying to extricate his arm. He hits Frank in the jaw with the back of his free hand and wrenches himself free.

'You fucker.'

Gordon lunges. Frank dodges and as his brother stumbles, drunk, off balance, Frank smacks him, firmly, on the side of the head. Four thick knuckles. Solid. Square. He falls like a stunned pig, sprawled on the rug.

'Pack it in, Gogs, before you get hurt.'

Gordon rises and takes another swing. He might not be fit, but he's heavy. His fist lands on Frank's shoulder and staggers him. Carol is up and makes a lunge for him, wrapping her arms around his neck, but he turns and shoves her against the sink with a crash. Frank's fist connects again, full face. He feels the nose go. The crunch of it. Gordon is down. Frank watches him on the kitchen floor, dazed, then Gordon clambers up, at last, and stands before him, breathing heavily. He wipes blood off his chin and looks at it with disgust. He walks to the kitchen table, opens the drawer and pulls out the gun. The Redhawk. He holds it in a shaking hand, pointing, moving it from one to the other.

Frank lifts his hands, appeasing his brother.

'Steady, Gordon.'

'Fuck you both.'

He turns to Frank.

'You can get back in that car and piss off back home.'

His shooting hand trembles. Frank can see his finger stroking the trigger. The gun moves from Carol to Frank and back again. Something croaks outside. Something answers back.

'Put it down, Gogs.'

'I'll do it. Believe me.'

'Jesus, Gordon.'

He has a ferocious look in his eyes, flint hard, crazy.

'Please Gordon,' says Carol.

He pulls up then, suddenly, and holds the gun in the flat of his upturned palm. Frank watches him. His brother knows the weight of an empty gun. He puts the barrel against her head and pulls the trigger. Frank flinches. There's just an idle click. Then click and click again. He raises the gun above her head, as if he means to bring it crashing down, but Frank has the neck of an empty cava bottle in his fist. It lights up the kitchen as it flies. It shatters on the side of Gordon's head and he's out.

wallsend - newcastle 1978

Laurence loosens his tie, pours tea from the teapot and looks over at Frank.

'How's our resident dog's-body this morning?' he asks.

'What?' says Frank.

Gordon sniggers and pours milk onto his cereal. Breakfast time at the Bridges, half seven on a Monday morning. Still dark outside. A toast rack and a jar of marmalade. The gas fire is blazing. Gordon is shovelling cereal into his mouth.

Laurence grabs the spoon in his son's fist and holds it still, over the bowl. 'Do you have to eat like a pig?'

Gordon waits stony-faced for his father to release his grip. The boy is implacable. When the grip relents Gordon continues slurping.

Laurence shakes his head. 'In the club yesterday you were bemoaning the lack of responsibility.'

Frank feels his throat tightening. His father's scrutiny is like a physical manifestation. Frank always feels it in the throat, as if he's being throttled.

'No I wasn't.'

Frank watches his father buttering his toast with slow, precise movements, every inch the same thin slathering of Stork. He cleans the blade of the knife on the edge of the toast, then dollops a spoonful of Golden Shred into the centre. Frank watches the same, careful appropriation of marmalade across the surface of toast. Laurence looks up and catches him watching. He pauses from eating.

'You're coming with me this morning.'

'Where?' asks Frank.

'To speak to Eddie's wife.'

Frank puts down his toast. 'Why?'

'You're going to explain what happened to her husband,' says Laurence. 'Since you want a bit more responsibility.'

'I don't know what happened, and I didn't say that.'

'I'll fill you in on the way over,' he says.

'I don't want to,' says Frank.

'I'm not asking, Lad. I'm telling.'

'I'll go,' says Gordon, sitting upright suddenly.

Laurence looks at him and snorts.

'Aye well, fuck yehs.'

Laurence stares at him and starts to say something, then lets it go. Gordon dips his head to the dark pool of his coco pops and stirs the milk.

'Do we have to?' Frank asks his father.

'It's a courtesy.'

'I'm sure she'll be fucking delighted,' says Frank.

With the palm of his hand, Laurence wallops him on the back of the head. Frank yells and stands up with his fists clenched, arms held firmly beside him. His father looks at them and laughs.

'Come on then, you little bender.'

Frank sits back down and looks at Gordon, who's bemused and entertained by proceedings now.

'Fine,' says Frank.

'Let's see what it's like at the sharp end, shall we?' says Laurence.

After breakfast they meet at the car. Laurence looks at Frank in his jeans and jacket and shakes his head.

'Not like that, son. Collar and tie for this.'

On the way back out the postman hands him a letter. Addressed to Francis Bridge. It must be his gran. No one calls him that. He sniffs the envelope. He's never had a letter before. He shoves it in his jacket pocket and gets in the car.

They drive in silence, Frank in his Sunday best. He pulls at the collar, loosening his tie, fiddling with his cuffs.

'Why are we doing this?' he asks.

'Like I said, it's a courtesy.'

'We're not gonna tell her that we had owt to do with it?'

'We're going to tell her the truth.'

'Jesus. Why?' asks Frank.

'She deserves to know. We're not in the business of cowardice. We're here to maintain ties. To manage business. The maintenance of order. It all needs to work like clockwork. One big family. When it gets out of kilter, it's a problem. I thought I could trust Eddie. I did trust Eddie. I can forgive many things. We all have our weaknesses. But when brass goes missing, that's the bottom line. Brass is our life blood, Frank. Without that, we're digging ditches and doffing our caps. It's a capital offence.'

Frank winds the window down, feels the cool air on his face. It's rush hour and the Wolseley crawls along, hemmed-in between a truck and a school bus that billows a thick blue cloud of diesel fumes into the air. On the back seat, a line of spotty teenage kids are giving them wanking gestures and two-finger salutes. Frank shakes his head. He thinks about Carol, laid in her bed, dreaming of God knows what. Is she alone? Gordon could have made it there by now. People wander by with their brollies up. The pavement glistens. Outside Marks & Sparks a black whippet pisses on a lamp post while its owner stands watching. Its back legs tremble as if from the cold. It turns and sniffs its piss and they wander on, the two of them. Women with shopping bags. Butchers opening, scrawny, pink carcasses hang in the windows. Ironmongers. A mirror shop with a hundred different mirrors reflecting the dark clouds back to themselves. A greengrocer, tables full of fruit and veg. The apples seem so red. Someone falls and picks themselves up.

When they get to her house, they stand in the front room, in the cold. It's like a museum. The best china stands gleaming in a glass cabinet, everything ordered and perfectly set. Mavis knows it's bad news. She knew it as soon as she clocked them on the doorstep. She stands shaking, wiping her hands on her pinny.

'It's about Eddie, isn't it?'

Laurence looks at Frank and nods him forwards.

Frank mutters, incoherently. He doesn't know what to say. He rubs his hands together, for warmth, or through a kind of abjection and awkwardness he's never known the likes of before. He feels his stomach churn and takes a deep breath.

'We, erm. We found him in Ashington, he—'

Her face begins to crumple. The lips quiver, but then she holds herself. She nods as if it's something she's been expecting for a long time. She looks at Frank, briefly, then looks at Laurence.

'He was a good man, Laurie,' she says. 'We just— Life isn't easy. He doesn't deserve this.'

'Maeve.'

She takes a deep breath. It's almost violent. Her eyes are shut.

'Was it you?'

It's almost a whisper. She walks over to Laurence and starts to beat him on the chest. She has to reach up her arm to do it, she's so small, and Laurence just stands there, unflinching, and then she starts weeping, her tears coming freely now, letting it out. Frank thinks about going to her, to hold her perhaps, but stands instead and watches, and then she stops and Laurence embraces her instead.

'I'm sorry, Maeve.'

'Laurence.'

She pulls away and wipes her eyes with a tissue and sits on the sofa. She seems a distant figure. Not the indomitable woman Frank remembers her as. Is this what grief does to you? Turns you into a shadow? She's grey. Withered.

'We've no gripe with you Maeve. You're well loved in these parts.'

He takes a well-stuffed envelope out of his pocket and lays it on the arm of the sofa.

'We'll let ourselves out.'

In the hallway, Jackie stands, chewing a sleeve of his jumper. He's looking through the open door towards his mother, his face wet with tears. He seems petrified. Laurence puts his hand on the child's head and ruffles his hair.

'Look after your mum, Jackie.'

They sit in the car and listen to the rain drum on the roof. It's a nice part of town, trees in the gardens. Frank is trying to calm down. His father is watching him. That scrutiny again. It cuts right through. But Laurence smiles and holds out his hand. Frank can't believe it. He's never shaken his father's hand. Never been offered it. He takes it and shakes. How firm the grip.

'That's the contract. It's how we maintain ties,' says Laurence. 'It's easy to walk off and turn your back, but that leads to weak links, disintegration. The end of business.'

They drive through the drab streets towards home. Progress is slow. Frank asks to be dropped off at the dockside. Maybe he'll see Carol down the Ship. When they pull up beside the water, they sit for a while looking out. The shadow of a great tanker is cast across the wharves.

'Frank.'

'What?'

'All this.'

'All this what?'

Laurence sighs. He seems disappointed by Frank's tone of voice.

'All this wealth, all this magnificence' – he pauses a moment, as if gathering his thoughts – 'All this hard fucking work. It's all yours, Frank. Or will be.'

Frank stares out of the window at the failing industry. All of it seizing up, arthritic. It won't be long now before it's over. Everyone knows it. His father refuses to see it. But there it is, none the less. He notices his father's shaking hand as he holds a cigarette. For a moment it seems as if he can't get the filter between his lips. Like he's nervous. It hovers around his mouth. *Bernie the Bolt,* thinks Frank, and then it's in and he's sucking hard. He turns to Frank and smiles and holds his hand out in front of him, the cigarette between index and second finger, trembling gently. Frank notes the worried look on Laurence's face.

'Cool Hand Luke,' his father says, and laughs, but the laugh is a bitter one.

'What is it, Dad?'

'Nothing. Just the bogeyman.'

Frank puts it down to too much booze in the club the night before, but years later, when his own hand trembles like this, suddenly, unexpectedly, he will think back to this moment and see what his father saw: something amiss in the DNA. The beginnings of something tragic. And then it's like Laurence has forgotten about his lecture and Frank gets out into the grey, drizzled light. He feels deflated, awkward in his suit and tie, his polished shoes. He looks like a spiv. No one's around, thank God, but still. Most of the town is hard at graft behind the walls, and those who aren't are still in bed, or down the job centre, signing on. The noise of the docks crashes in his head. He finds an abandoned berth and sits on one of the old rusting cleats, among the weeds and clutter. He thinks about Mrs Armstrong again. His father was right, they'd done the proper thing, but he can't feel it, not in his bones, and now that the buzz has worn off, all the energy seems to have gone out of him. He takes the letter out of his pocket and tears it open. It's from Carol. He has a dreadful feeling that all isn't well. He goes through it twice. A long rambling letter full of dreams and nonsense: how she loves him and always will, but that she and Gordon are getting married and leaving town. A long line of kisses along the bottom.

newcastle city centre

Shoulder to shoulder on Percy Street they march; the faithful, decked in black and white. The great crowd bays. A river of men, out of the citadel, owning the city they live in, claiming it, as they do every Saturday, or every other Saturday, as the fixtures foretell. Above them the great stanchions of the Gallowgate stand like a fort on an ancient earthwork. A place of worship. And the floodlights light up the sky with the mimic of daylight. They're coming down from the hallowed turf. A bad afternoon: routed in their own home, by apostates. The natural order has been usurped. Now all they need is the sacrificial lamb. In the city centre they hunt it down. The shout goes up – 'Mackems' – and a torrent of bricks and chunks of breeze block shatter on the road, bottles and beer glasses. Windscreens disintegrate. Shop windows fall into the street. 'Geordie cunts,' comes the taunt. The ugly blur of red and white, smeared against the elegant Georgian facades of Grey Street. They stand across the road from each other, taunting, jabbing fingers, chanting obscenities, and Carol stands, front and centre, bold as Boudica, goading them, gesturing one and all to come and touch the cloth.

Missiles fly, a chair comes through the window of the pub and then it's all in, across the border of hostilities. Bar stools swing like battering rams. Frank feels a blow to the side of his jaw and down he goes, a boot in the chest. Carol drags him up and out, like a wounded soldier. It's music to his ears, symphonic, the way it fills him. The buzz. The rush of adrenaline. He sits on the steps of a newsagent getting his breath. His jaw hurts, his chest feels battered. The sirens of police cars echo off the grand avenues. Van after van. The pigs file out and get stuck in themselves to the red and white. Unwelcome visitors in this town of theirs. Cheers go up at the baton charge, the barking of dogs, the clatter of horse hooves on tarmac. The Toon Army stands back and lets the coppers have a good go at the scum. Cheering them on, for once. When they've been dispersed and rounded up, all that's left is to scour the alleys and pubs for stragglers: the lost, the ignorant, the stupid. They head back across town, Frank and Carol and Gordon, arm in arm. Eddie Armstrong swinging a metal pipe. They find a bunch of them hanging out in China-town, munching noodles from foil trays, twenty or so. They've taken off their colours, hidden them, or chucked them, but as soon as they see the black and white they drop their chow mein and flee en masse in the vague direc-tion of the station. They've no idea where they're going and are kettled out towards West Walls and the bottleneck there, to be crucified against the medieval stone. Those that fall are kicked to a pulp and the others chased deeper and deeper into Pink Lane and the alleys where the warehouses stand, blind and indifferent.

There's no escape as they pile in. Boots and fists, railing posts, scaffolding. Anything they can get their hands on that's hard and damaging. The infidel can hear the tantalising chorus of their kith, gathered in safety at the central station, *Sunderland, Sunderland, Sunderland*, but they are beyond appeal, there is no help coming. The city wall stands fifteen feet above the passage and Frank watches one of them getting his face scraped along the stonework, a smear of blood and skin. *Kill the Mackems.* He sees Gordon swing his heavy knuckled fist into a face. He winces at the thought. The guy hits the deck and smacks his head on a kerbstone, he's dazed and falls back, but then he rises and lunges at Gordon. Frank sees the flash of steel and his brother falls. Carol has half a house brick in her hand which comes down savagely on the back of the man's head and sends him sprawling in the gutter. She bends to Gordon then, and gathers him in and holds him. They've brought blades, the low lives. Frank kneels at his brother's side. He's clutching a stomach wound. The alley empties as the fracas moves on. The red and white back off towards the church and the stone grows quiet. Gordon is laid on the path, laughing.

'You daft sod. He could have killed you,' says Carol.

Frank unzips his brother's jacket, pulls up his shirt. A nasty gash in the waist, running blood. Could have been worse. It isn't much. Silence envelops them for a moment.

He can smell the ancient stone, the wall, built to keep bar-barians at bay. Shattered glass lies everywhere. When he stands, it crunches beneath his boots. A baking spud lies on the floor, studded with razor blades. Frank pulls him to his feet.

'How you feeling?'

'I'm alright, brother.'

'We should get you to the General.'

'Fuck that. I'm alright.'

'Pub then.'

Gordon has an arm around Frank's shoulder as they stagger like drunks down to the County, Carol ahead of them looking for Mackems. She's all wound up and ready for a fight. She's worse than Gordon; they're like some monstrous two-headed dog on these Saturday afternoons.

You can hear the Mackems singing in the station, boarding trains, heading back to their hovels on the Wear. Their hymns rise high and loud into the platform roofing. A foreign language. Horse shit covers the roads and pavements, match programmes, smashed glass. A shoe. A scattering of red and white hats lies forlornly on the tarmac.

They flop into the bar and take a seat by the window. It's heaving. Frank takes a copy of the *Pink* off the window ledge to check the scores, but all he can see is the scoreline from St James's Park. Two fucking nil. It leaves a bitter taste in his Guinness. Liverpool top. That's alright. He hates the colours, but he doesn't mind the Scousers. Shankly. Looks like his fucking grandad. Gordon groans and shifts in his seat. He'll live. Frank turns towards him and sees his jeans turning a dark and bloody red. Gordon looks up and catches him. He shakes his head.

'Fuck off, Frank.'

They sit in the hot bar, among the throng of their own tribe. And Frank sees Carol throw her arms around Gordon and kiss him, full on the mouth, and she's beaming. God, how she loves match day and all its buzz. In the County it's like church: meaningful, ceremonial. There's singing and chanting and not a little wailing, scuffles and fights, and disagreements over the merits or otherwise of Hibbitt and Cassidy. And Gordon, bleeding, clambers onto his seat, then onto the rickety table and stands, fleet-footed among the drinks in his winklepickers, and starts conducting the lunatics, the mad choristers, in renditions of the 'Blaydon Races': 'Ah me lads, ye shudda seen wi gannin', We pass'd the foaks alang the road just as they wor stannin', Thor wis lots o' lads an' lassies there, aal wi' smiling faces, Gannin' alang the Scotswood Road, to see the Blaydon Races.'

When he sits back down and slumps in his seat, he's sweating. Carol reaches across and puts her palm against his wound. He yelps in pain.

'I think we need to get him to the hospital,' she says to Frank, but Gordon tells her to fuck off and to get him another pint.

Frank lets his brother slump against him.

'Fucking stabbed you, Gogs.'

'Fuck it.'

'You not scared of dying?'

'I'm not scared of anything.'

His little brother is a nutcase. Inured to the notion of suffering. Carol laughs and ruffles Frank's hair.

'You're a soft bugger, Frank,' she says.

They're onto their fifth pint, and it's dark outside. A moment of peace. Of solitude among the mayhem. Frank looks out through the cut-glass window and sees it fall through the night, like a meteorite. It's lit by the street-lights, a ball bearing, small as a gobstopper, come from the hand of a heretic. It shines like a star. He sees it in slow motion. It hits dead centre and the surface of the great window shivers like a membrane. It bends and billows, and then it gives with a whoosh and glass blows through the pub, like sand. A vicious wind comes in and sucks at their scarves. A cheer goes up from the multitude, from the paralytic congregation. Gordon doesn't flinch. He flicks the glass off his shoulders, looks at his pint and, seeing no foreign bodies there, downs it in one.

sierra de cádiz 2003

Gordon is face down on the kitchen flagstones. Out cold. Frank yanks open the cellar door. Cool air sweeps over him. Down in the darkness are stone steps, a wooden rail. There's a switch inside the door. He snaps it on and a weak yellow light flickers into life. He turns back to his brother, takes his ankles and drags him along the kitchen floor, but Gordon is coming round, moaning, muttering incomprehensible things at the floor. He's impossible to shift. The kitchen rug ruffles up beneath him and his legs start to twist in protestation. Arms start pulling in the opposite direction. It's a seesaw. Frank manages, somehow, to get him into the doorway, the head of the cellar steps. Gordon calls his name. A beast waking from slumber. His hands find the broken cava bottle, and he grasps it, tight, like it might just save his life.

'Frank,' he groans.

A voice full of pain. Pathetic. It tugs at Frank's heart. Every second Gordon is more fully conscious.

'Frank, please.'

Frank pulls as hard as he can, the dead weight of his brother, and gets him down finally to the cool cellar floor.

The place is lined with shelf after shelf of wine bottles, jars of orange marmalade glowing gold, plums in syrup: the bounty of her garden. He pulls Gordon deeper inside, hops over him, back up the stairs and closes the door. Locks it.

Carol is leaning against the wall, her mouth bleeding where Gordon struck her. She has a cut hand from a broken glass on the draining board. He kneels beside her and studies the wound.

'You alright, Caz?'

'I think so.'

He stands to get the med kit from a kitchen cabinet and finds an antiseptic wipe, a few sticking plasters. He sits back down beside her and wipes the cut on her finger, wraps a plaster tight around the wound.

'You took the bullets out!'

'I did.'

'I thought we were dead.'

He pulls her close and hugs her. He can feel her heart beating against his chest. They cling until their breathing settles. He gets to his hands and knees and looks for the gun. It's under the table. He picks it up and spins the chamber.

'He loves that gun.'

'What the hell does he use it for?'

'Target practice usually: cans, bottles, goats.'

'Goats?'

'Anything.'

'Jesus. Where are the shells?'

'In the Tupperware, under the sink.'

Frank finds it and opens it up. He fills the cylinder. Snaps it in place and lays the gun beside him on the floor. He sits by her and fishes two cigarettes out of the packet in his shirt pocket. They sit in the quiet on the hard stone floor and smoke in silence. It soothes him.

Soon Gordon starts banging on the cellar door, cursing: cunts, fuckers, bastards, wankers. He promises to break down the door and snap their fucking necks and cut their throats. A furious volley of cracks against the solid wood. Frank rises and goes to the door. He gives it a kick.

There's a pause.

'Fuck you. I'm gonna kill you when I get out of here. And I'm gonna kill her too.'

'No, Gordon. You're not,' and a tremor goes through him.

Gordon resumes his ferocious hammering at the door. Frank takes Carol's hand and leads her outside, into the peace and quiet. A breeze blows from somewhere, so sweet it is almost overwhelming.

heaton - newcastle 2002

The nursing home has seen better times. How did he end up here? King of the Tyne slumming it in his last days? Must have got it cheap. That wouldn't surprise him, hoarder of all he has, miser, tight-fisted cunt. The staff are fabulous, kindly and accommodating; would they like tea and biscuits brought in? Their smiles are heartbreaking. Laurence's room is almost monastic. He's laid in his single bed, sheets and blankets, not the comfort of an airy duvet; no he's tucked up tight, and who can blame them. Frank feels weary today. Anxious at finding himself back in Newcastle. He sits in the chair beside the bed.

'Hello, Dad.'

Laurence is staring at the ceiling, perfectly still. He doesn't have long now, they told him at the desk, a week or two at most. They're not a hospital, but the doctor comes around each day.

'Dad,' he says, but nothing. A rattle in the chest. A rattle snake. A sigh. Perhaps of resignation. Perhaps of disappointment that he can't actually die in peace and has to endure the presence of his son as he slips away. Frank feels incapacitated again. Inhibited. He feels a need to talk, but what can he say? What does he want the answers to? He's not sure. He studies his father's face, gaunt now, the sunken cheeks, the pitiful rise and fall of his chest. The eyes are open but what does he see?

Frank turns from his father and stands at the window overlooking the carpark. The dereliction, the broken glass, row after row of anonymous cars. Behind the tea factory someone walks his dog, a greyhound, across the concrete. A bus heads over a distant bridge. Imagine, the very last thing you see before slipping away, the final image you carry off into oblivion, the flickering tail end of a movie, fading to black. His father is staring still at the ceiling, a yellow stain above his bed; the tiniest stalactite hangs from an incrustation of salt. Is that what he sees? If he sees at all. He thinks about his visit, only last summer, to Keats's house, on the Spanish Steps in Rome. The poet's death bed – *the phlegm seemed boiling in his throat* – a window onto the clear, blue Roman sky. The beautiful ceiling covered in flowers. It took all of Frank's effort to stop from weeping. Was that the image that Keats took with him to the grave? What was the last thing Lorca saw, he wonders, before they put a bullet in him.

He goes back to his chair. He'd like to leave, but he doesn't want them to think he doesn't care. 'He's a good son. He stayed with his dying father for hours in the silence, in the gathering dark,' they will say. He wonders then about Gordon. How he would feel. There was no love lost between them, but still, when your father dies, it is no small thing.

When Laurence turns his head suddenly and looks at Frank, it's a shock. His father grins at him and Frank feels the hairs on his neck prickle.

'Dad. Can you talk?'

Nothing. Another sigh. Frank always imagined a lavish nursing home looking out onto grand gardens, the sound of birdsong coming in; peacocks maybe. Not for his father, but for himself. Laurence had no appreciation of rural beauty. Or any other kind. There's nothing for Frank here. No victory. No surcease. He knows he should feel something – sorrow, regret, sympathy, hate – but he can't manage it. He feels empty. He needs to go. At the door he takes a last look at his father. The great Laurence Bridge.

a screening (super 8)

They set up the screen and settle in a hush, in the dark, waiting for the house projectionist, Mum, to feed the film through the sprockets and holes and set the past in motion. They stare at their own ghosts, in a washed-out, sublimated palate that they all believe is the actual colour of the past, the pastel blues and muted reds and dusty greens. There's no sound, just the rattle of stock through the gate, a steady, hypnotising flutter, as snow comes down on Town Moor, and the boys, Francis and Gordon, bomb towards the camera on a red sledge, closer, closer, bigger. Gordon is in front and Frank behind, his arms wrapped around his brother's neck, eyes shut, as if in fear of the future. If you could stop it right there, freeze frame, and study the tableaux, you'd see them amid the snowstorm, delirious in their happy moment, Frank's head thrown back, Gordon focused. The sledge caught mid-plummet as it hurtles towards the camera. The snow falls relentlessly on everything, so white you could almost be anywhere, places no one has ever heard of before – Kyoto, Anchorage, Oslo – not deep in the heart of this pit-wasted land, this coal-black town. For a moment all is still, composed. Someone, right at the edge of the frame, almost unnoticed and certainly unknown, wanders with his dog somewhere. You wouldn't ever see him at normal speed. This is how things are. Somewhere nobody knows you, nobody sees you. And still the sledge is looming, caught between two worlds. Wind on, run the film. A blister bubbles on the celluloid, pops, then disappears. You can hear the scream, though there isn't one, just a room full of laughter as the sledge hits, and the camera falls in the snow. 'Sack the bloody cameraman!' someone shouts from the back. As someone does every Christmas. As the camera is recovered and the button pressed, the scene continues. A jumble of bodies laid in the deep drifts, scattered but unharmed, and Gordon, the first to rise, victorious, intrepid sledge pilot, stands looking camera-wards and laughing. He stick two fingers up and makes a silent howl into the snowflakes. 'Cheeky monkey,' says old Grandma Bridge, as she says every Christmas, as if she's seeing it for the first time, which in a way she is, since year on year she seems to remember less and less and the world gets emptier and more beautiful with every passing day. You can see Gordon crouch into the deep drifts to retrieve his brother buried in snow, and they stand together, unsteady on their feet. They dust each other off and their laughter is infectious, though you cannot hear it. They turn and talk silently to someone behind the camera – Mum – and wander off, the two of them, hand in gloved hand, pulling the sledge up the hill into falling snow until they almost disappear. And then they do.

sierra de cádiz 2003

It's almost cool in the bedroom. A thin cotton sheet covers them.

'Can you turn the light out, Frankie?' She turns away when he looks at her. 'I hate looking like this.'

He studies her face, turns it to the light. A bruise on her cheek. Her cut lip. The black eye, fading now.

'Got away with one there,' he says.

He leans over and turns off the bedside lamp. They lie beneath the cool draught of the ceiling fan as it whirrs and shushes above them. She turns to face him. He can just see her in the gloom. She has a hand on his leg, warm and tender, and he reaches out for her in the dark: her thigh, her stomach, her breast. There's still that hesitancy he felt in the garden. He wants to hold her but he's not sure how. How does Carol feel? So many years have passed them by, so many questions. He likes the touch of her. The softness of flesh. Its heat. She's fuller than she used to be, less firm, sags in all the right places. A bit like himself now. The long haul of years. He puts his lips to a nipple. It grows in his mouth.

'Is this all right?' she whispers.

'Yes.'

It's simpler than either of them imagines. She breathes deeply. Sometimes you just let go, and see. They move slowly, older now, hesitant, like pensioners in the act of love. They have a trusting, familiar way with one another. How long has it been? They exchange only expletives, which are whispered into the air, disembodied words of encouragement, or pleasure. And then it is over and he flops beside her, holding her hand. It was pleasant enough, but he feels oddly ashamed. Sad. He pulls her towards him and kisses her.

'And Judah said unto Onan, Go in unto thy brother's wife, and marry her, and raise up seed to thy brother,' says Frank, and he laughs.

'Is that the Bible?'

'It is.'

'Seed,' she repeats in the darkness.

They both laugh. He nuzzles at her neck, then lies on his back.

She's soon asleep. He can smell her grapey breath, hear her soft snores. He lies in the dark and drifts in and out of sleep beneath the ever-turning fan. A liminal, haunted world of shadows. Of turmoil and bloodshed. A night full of moans and pleadings. A vivid but nebulous dream of violence. When he does sleep it is fleeting, or just under the surface, and he jolts awake and sees that the stars have shifted in the windowpane. At other times he surfaces but cannot wake, and stares at the bedroom walls as if through a thin membrane.

When he wakes for the last time, in the middle of the night, it's like he's been woken at sea. He's disoriented. Carol snores quietly, contentedly. He looks at her bedside clock. It's already four. He can see the moon, white as ice in a pool of gin. *Doña Luna. A butterfly could puff you out.* He slips out of bed, surprised to find he still has his boxers on. She's under the covers. Oblivious. He wraps a towel around his waist, empties the glass of water beside his bed and heads downstairs, past the cellar door to the kitchen. The beast is quiet in its lair. He puts his ear to the wooden door and hears a deep snoring. It's like a fairy tale. He steps outside into the blue air. Unworldly. Beautiful. Warm. He walks to his car and opens the door and gets inside, sits in the deep leather seats. He touches the pedals, grips the wheel. All he really has to do is turn the keys and go. Chuck it all. But how can he? It's too hot in the car. He gets out and sits on a lounger. The stars struggle to hold their own against the brilliant moon. There's a milkiness to the sky. The pool lies limpid, turquoise and inviting. Among the vines a solitary light bulb shines. A cloud of insects devours the light; moths and mosquitoes mass at the bulb, a dizzy scribble. Down the coast a string of lights twinkles. A different world. He watches with a kind of longing. He never wakes at this time. This is special. Both magical and terrifying. A secret segment of night.

He stands at the pool's edge, his toes curling over the tiles. He bends at the knee and dives into the cooling water. It takes his breath away in a flurry of bubbles. He rises. He turns and lies on his back, the north star above him, dead centre of everything. The star they sailed the ships by. He goes over the whole fiasco. Gordon, uncontrollable, murderous. Carol's stunning act of provocation. How to come back from that? He gets a sinking feeling in his belly. He should never have come. He should have done things differently. It's too late now. That terrifying click of the trigger. Thank God she took the shells out. This is not the end of it. He can barely think about what happens next.

kielder forest - northumberland 1979

Frank sits in the passenger seat beside Dawn. The window is open and he listens to the rain dripping through the trees, a steady tick-tock. The floor of the forest is a matting of moss and leaf mulch. It seems to suck the moisture out of the air. Cold for a summer's day, and miserable. He watches their breath billow and mingle in the car, then drift and vanish. Mist appears and disappears in swathes. He listens to her bored sighs and sniffs the pine, the Sitka spruce, stacked as they are, one against the other, for fifty miles around. There must be millions of them. It clears the nostrils, the airways. He looks at his watch and fidgets.

'Stop fidgeting, Frank.'

This is the loneliest place. Far from home. He's running plans through in his head. He just hopes the boys can manage a simple job without screwing up. He wouldn't bet on it. Laurence had told him: 'Keep it simple.' Prove your mettle. Straight in and straight out. He looks at Gordon and Macca, smoking beside the track, acting the goat. Liabilities, the both of them. God knows why Laurence has asked him to gaffer the job, it's the last thing he wants. And why these two nut jobs? It just makes things harder. He wonders if his father is losing the plot. It should be a simple job: highjack the van after its last post office pick-up, an isolated stretch of road near the Scottish border. Get the driver and his mate into the Rover, and bring the whole lot down here, into the forest. Out of sight.

He takes Dawn's hand and grips it. Why did he bring her, he wonders. It's just one more complication. He wants to show Carol. That's why. Show her she's made a mistake. He puts his head back against the seat and takes a deep breath. He can see one of the cars ahead: Paddy's, obscured by the trees. Paddy's OK. Has a wife and kids. Plays things straight. Cigarette smoke drifts from one of its windows. Gordon's car is somewhere on the other side, obscured by trees. They wait. He listens to the drops of water fall on the roof of the car. Everything ticks and sucks and drinks. If you didn't know better you might think you were fish, living under water: the green light, the shifting shadows. The world seen through a jam jar full of pond water. He keeps glancing in the rearview mirror. He's more nervous than he should be. Eventually he sees the distant dots of headlights. He stubs out his cigarette and opens his door. The Rover pulls up just in front of him and the van driver and his mate are bundled out. They stand, bedraggled, on the side of the track as the van turns up.

The boys appear like spectres out of the dark, their guns pointing at the guys.

'Stop here, Dawn.'

He leans across and kisses her on the cheek, a peck. Pathetic. He hates himself. The guys have their hands raised. Frank wanders over towards them. They look nervous.

'Don't worry,' he tells them. 'Just keep your noses clean and no one gets hurt.'

'Where's the keys?' says Welby to the driver.

'We don't have the keys. We don't have access to the vault.'

He's telling the truth. Safer for the company that way. Frank explained all this before they left Newcastle, but they've forgotten already. Or don't care to remember. Gordon approaches the driver and strikes him with his rifle stock, on the side of the head. It sends him sprawling.

'Pack it in,' shouts Frank. The others gather round, jostling, full of nervous energy. Paddy lifts the driver to his feet. Welby dusts the dirt off the man's uniform, then head-butts him. Laughter. The man falls again to the ground.

'Where's the fucking keys, dick?'

'They don't have the keys, now tie them up and get to work on the vault,' Frank says.

'I don't pissing believe it,' moans Gordon.

The driver's mate bends down to help his colleague to his feet, his nose bloodied and broken. Welby shoves him, and stupidly – Frank can't believe it – the man pushes back at Welby, hard, sending him backwards into the muddy track. He slips and falls on his arse. The men start laughing, which riles Welby and then the driver's mate thinks this is a good moment to run for the trees. Gordon's gun cracks the silence and the man falls. The driver calls out his name. A scuffle begins, and then there's a barrage of gun shots, smoke and sparks and a wild, terrifying echo through the trees. Frank fires a barrel off, high above them. They all duck, instinctively and turn towards him. When the echoes die and the birds are stilled into silence, the driver by the truck is a mass of torn holes, his company uniform smoking in the breeze.

'What the fuck?'

'Christ,' says Gordon.

'You morons,' shouts Frank.

'They asked for it,' says Gordon, 'they were coming for us.'

Frank backhands his brother across the face, splitting his lip. Gordon shoves him in the chest then turns away, fingering his bloody mouth.

'Weren't even armed, Gogs.'

'It just kicked off,' says Welby.

Frank lets out a loud, frustrated groan and wanders back to the car. He sits with Dawn while the boys get the welding gear out, the gas tanks and cutters. His hands are shaking. He thumps the steering wheel in frustration. Thumps it again. Dawn is terrified. She's shaking. What has he done?

'I'm sorry,' he says. 'I shouldn't have brought you.'

She manages, with shaking hands, to light up a cigarette and sucks on it, deeply.

'He's trouble, that brother of yours,' she manages to say.

'Tell your fucking sister that,' he says, and regrets it as soon as its out of his mouth. What's the matter with him? He shakes his head. The car is filled with a perfume he's unfamiliar with. He steals a glance at her. She's calming down. She blows smoke through the open window then looks down the long beam of the headlights into the darkness. Different to Carol. Less mutinous. More submissive. He likes mutinous. Whatever dumb plan he had bringing her here has disappeared in the gun smoke. He looks away. In the wing mirror he can see them working. Their vague shapes and shadows. The turquoise flame of the acetylene torch glows in the dark, like a wood sprite, intense and vivid. He checks his watch. Plenty of time, but still, they need to move. It takes an hour with the welding gear. When he hears the cheer, he gets out and joins them. They've got through the roof and have the back doors open. A stack of mail sacks and a pile of safe-deposit boxes. He cuts one of the sacks open. Neat bundles. Twenties.

'OK. Get them into Gordon's car and everyone sod off home. If I was you, I'd keep your fucking heads down for a while.'

He watches them carry the stuff to his brother's car and they all drive away. Except for Gordon. His engine is idling at the side of the track, releasing its sickly monoxide into the trees. Frank walks over and knocks on the window. Gordon winds it down. He has a bundle of twenties in his hand and is flicking them over, like a pack of cards.

'That was a fuck-up back there, Gogs.'

'So what?'

'I can't be bailing you out every time we go out on a job.'

'Well.'

'Well what?'

Gordon holds the bundle of notes up to his nose and smells them. He grins broadly.

'Put it back.'

'Here. Take it. You're the boss. You deserve a tip.'

He thrusts the money towards him.

'Later, Gordon. We'll all get a split. Now get the fuck out of here.'

Gordon sits back in his seat. He sighs, deeply.

'What's up? We need to get moving.'

He looks into Frank's eyes, then looks away. 'Sorry, Frank.'

'What?'

'I'll see you around.'

'What the fuck you talking about?'

'I'm off, Frank. You'll never see me again.'

Frank tries the handle, but the door is locked. Gordon lifts a revolver and points it at Frank. He looks down at the barrel stuck against his coat, then back at the face of his brother. He feels suddenly the bitter cold of the woods.

'Gordon.'

'Don't come looking for me.'

'Where the—'

'I mean it.'

'Don't do this to me, Gogs.'

'You'll be alright. Just blame it on your dumb fucking brother, they'll understand.'

He drops two bundles on the road, beside Frank's boots, settles into first and pulls away. Frank watches him go with a sense of foreboding, watches until the red tail lights disappear from view. He bends and picks up the money.

He takes a moment to look around. They've probably left prints all over the place. He should clean everything down. Torch it. Can he be arsed? Can he fuck. A fine drizzle falls through the trees. It lights up the woods. The smell of pine is intoxicating. He stands beside the van. It looks like an old sardine can, its roof torn open. He looks down a long green corridor of trees that leads into darkness. The track is covered in pinecones, like unexploded hand grenades. A prophecy of conflict. Of bloodshed. Jesus Christ, Gordon. That's a tonne of cash. Laurence is going to go ballistic. The whole fucking lot of them. He wonders if Gordon's got the balls for it? The nous? He doubts it. This can only end badly. He looks at the guy on the roadside. It fills him with rage. What a fuckup. He turns back to his car. Dawn sits pale in the windscreen. It's like she's seen a ghost. Or a premonition of something tragic.

sierra de cádiz 2003

The next evening they wander from room to room, seeking peace, a cool, quiet spot, but find none. Finally they retire to the terrace in the stifling heat. They can just hear the faint cries, the distant smashing of bottles as the beast howls in its basement. It's been a whole day and a night now. They eat from the garden. The best tomatoes Frank has ever tasted, rich and fleshy, peppery courgettes, sweet, astringent onions. Carol has dressed the salad with a mustard vinaigrette. Pomegranate pips crunch pleasingly as he chews. She's halfway through a bottle of Amontillado, and who can blame her. The olives are intense and deeply flavoured. The cicadas have grown quiet at last and the crickets have taken their turn in the moonlight. Humming. A gentler, more melodious sound.

She reaches for his hand across the table.

'I shouldn't have told him about us.'

'There never was an us, Caz. It was always you and Gordon. I was surplus to requirements.'

He's surprised by the bitterness in his voice.

'That's not true, Frankie.'

'I could never understand what you saw in him. I still can't fathom it.'

Bubbles rise from the depths of the pool and pop on the surface. It shimmers, a turquoise glow in the still night.

'Gordon was different, back then,' she says. 'You must remember. A mental case for sure. He was wild, but not nasty. And I saw a different side to him. A sensitive side. We were both so young: nineteen, twenty when we first came here. We travelled all around Spain until we found this place. It was romantic. On the run, like Bonnie and Clyde. Still on the run, even now. But he's turned into something I don't recognise. He frightens me now.'

He watches her take a long drink of cold sherry, then carefully top up her glass.

'What do we do now?

Frank bows his head.

'We can't let him out,' she says.

'I know,' is the best he can offer.

He feels goosebumps rise on his arms despite the heat. He gazes over the landscape, the nebulous, tranquil groves, and sees again, with a heavy heart, the twinkling lights on the distant coast. He yearns for escape, to be free of obligation. But that's not possible any more. Whatever they've set in motion has changed everything.

He smokes as he listens to her talk. She's drunk and discursive. They drift into silence, the two of them thoughtful, close in the enveloping night air.

'I need to lie down, Frankie. My head's spinning. I drank too much.'

He tells her to go up, while he clears the table. She stumbles up the stairs with a clatter as he settles dishes and plates into the sink. They can sort this out in the morning. When he gets upstairs she's already asleep. He lies in his brother's bed again and lets the warmth of her naked body lull him. *The glory of booze*, he thinks. How he misses the drink. Perhaps he'll take it up again after all. He used to love that feeling of being so drunk that you fell asleep as soon as you hit the sack. Even so, his head is spinning. He closes his eyes, but he can't sleep. The past. The present. It all coagulates into one appalling mess. He imagines Gordon in the cellar. His own flesh and blood. 'Like peas in a pod,' his gran used to say, when they were bairns. He knows what has to be done and he can't bear it. He runs through every option, but it always returns to the same recourse. He looks at the moon again through the open window. Full now. The night of the madmen. The lunatic moon. Dragging at the body of water that makes up the man. Pulling the blood up his veins. Filling his head. From savage, to civilised man, then back to savage again. You can try, but you can never outrun yourself. He'd always thought that he could. These last decades, this running, this vain attempt to change. And now this. He's no better than he ever was. He looks at Carol sleeping. He gets out and sits on the side of the bed. He gets back in, pulls the thin white sheet over them both, but once again he cannot settle. All night the demons visit. If he sleeps, he dreams of a grey, rain-drenched home. The terraced houses, the glum, dejected bleakness. His mum, his gran. Whatever happens, you suffer. Everyone does. He remembers that afternoon in the woods. The last time Frank had seen his brother. The look on his face when he backhanded him.

wallsend - newcastle 1979

'His days are numbered. I will find him and I will skin the cunt.'

Laurence is raving. He paces up and down the room, his face contorted. Spittle flies from his mouth. He punches his palm with a loud smack.

Laurence turns on him. 'And as for you, I'll tear your fucking head off. We've been here before. We had this fucking self-same lecture after Eddie. This is ten times worse. The shame. It's unbearable. Family on fucking family. The cunt took off and you just stood there and let it happen.

'You' – he jabs his finger in Frank's chest – 'You're in on it.'

Frank can only shake his head. He's terrified of his father's anger, his capacity for sudden violence. It reminds him of Gordon. Incendiary. Volatile. They're cut from the same cloth. There's no calming him. He turns and leans on the dining-room table. Hyperventilating.

'I was gobsmacked,' Frank manages to say, 'I thought he was joking.'

He doesn't mention how Gordon turned the gun on him. How the barrel felt pressing against his chest.

'Fucking runt. You should have shot him. Put the fucker down. I don't understand you, Frank. I put you in charge.' He speaks in barely a whisper now. 'I trusted you, and you do this to me.'

'Dad.'

'Where is he?'

'I wish I knew.'

'You tell me, Frank. Or you're out.'

'Out?'

Frank can't believe what he's hearing.

'I can't protect you from what's coming. There's a lot of very angry men out there. They want their money, or they want their pound of flesh. Probably both. I can only do so much. You know what these people are like. They'll get to you one way or another.'

'You don't honestly believe I had anything to do with this, Dad.'

'It doesn't matter what I think.'

Frank's hands are shaking. Already he's wondering where he can go. When he should go. He looks at the two bundles of twenties that Gordon dropped for him, which are now standing on the dining room table. He may as well have taken the cash himself, got in beside Gordon and driven off with him. With him and Carol, like old time-gangsters. The three of them. He sees his father take a gun from inside his jacket and he feels the pelt rise on his neck. He's never seen his father with a gun. Everyone has them, but Laurence? Never. He checks the chamber. Slides it back into his pocket and stands in the middle of the room, breathing deeply. *What is he thinking?* Frank has shrunk. He feels lost, let go of suddenly.

'I need to go out. I need to calm a few tempers. This is all very difficult.'

He turns to Frank then, a look of disgust on his face. Frank can barely look him in the eyes.

'I suggest you lock the doors and don't answer to anyone. For your own safety.'

After Laurence goes out, he does what he's told. The silence in the house is terrifying.

wylam - northumberland 1979

His grandmother's garden is a ferment. It's good to be out in the country, among strangers, away from Newcastle. The heatwave continues without letting up. A garden party, a booze-up. Searing heat has left the village gasping. All across the North East the pubs are heaving and the clubs are running dry. Standpipes dribble on every street corner. Now the locals descend on the house with crates and bottles, party packs and home brew. A trestle table is set up under the crab apple tree. Grandma and the ladies from the WI have piled it with pies and stotties, hard-boiled eggs and homemade pickles. Meats are laid out, ham, beef and chicken. There's cheese and quiche, and a pile of paper plates teeters on the edge of the table. Frank stands before the feast and casts his eyes over the food. He screws the top off an old sweet jar and reaches in for a pickled egg. Coriander seeds float on the vinegar top as he pulls one out, large, grotesque and brown as leather brogues. He bites off the end and chews the firm flesh. It puckers his cheeks. He piles up his plate and takes a seat under the back porch.

He'll hide out at his gran's for a day or two. The

atmosphere in Wallsend is febrile. There's a lot of anger and the finger is being pointed at him, as Laurence had warned. It was him and Gordon both. Gordon couldn't plan a kid's birthday party, let alone a job like this. They must have planned it together. Laurence can only keep things chilled for so long; eventually they'll nobble him, for sure. He can't care any more. No option now, but to scarper, for good. Somewhere he can disappear. London most likely.

His gran's house is up the Tyne Valley, near Wylam, where the tide, when it rushes in, gives up the ghosts and settles accounts with the local fresh water. It is set in greenery, tight on the river, almost the wilds of Northumberland. He's loved the place since childhood, when he spent his summers here. Back then it held a great mystery. The way a landscape does for a child: so huge, the strange woods and dells, the ever-fascinating river banks, with its coterie of frogs and newts and quick, brown water rodents.

'Where is that brother of yours?'

Frank puts down his plate and stands to hug his gran. She holds him back at arm's length, to study him. Her eyes narrow. Her old irises, grey as hardboard pinheads.

'I wish I could tell you, Gran.'

'The poor lad.'

'He'll be alright.'

'He's far too sensitive, that boy.'

She wipes her hands on her pinafore in the age-old way, or perhaps like Pontius Pilate, she's washing her hands clean of all the familial nastiness.

'Your cousin Lucía is here,' she says.

'Who is that?'

'You'll see. You can't really miss her.'

She checks the table, the food and drink, then turns and wanders back to the kitchen.

From a bedroom window a stereo is pounding out 'Anarchy in the UK'. A deep heavy bass behind the mocking voice of Johnny Rotten: *I am an antichrist, I am an anarchist*. Mad Malc is pogoing with some girl Frank doesn't know, bouncing up and down like lunatics in the shadow of the house. Malcolm's hair rises in a bright blue, spiky comb, like a rooster. He watches them for a moment. They seem oblivious. In a world of their own making. They're on something more than good humour or booze, and Frank wishes for a moment he could live life like that. He isn't taken by the music though. He prefers Black Sabbath and King Crimson. Frank wanders away down the long garden, closer to the river.

On the steps of an old broken-down gazebo his grandad sits in his chair drinking a glass of stout. Beside him an old, weathered man with a hat is picking at some battered guitar. A cigarette hangs from his mouth. As he gets closer he can hear the crazy flourishes of his fingers against the copper-coloured strings. They seem to glow in the sunlight. It isn't like any music he's heard before. He stands with a beer, watching the old raven-headed man flicking and picking and striking occasionally the wooden body of his old guitar. No one who sits nearby is anything other than spellbound. Frank looks back up the garden towards the house. His uncle Brendan sitting in the shade, smoking a pipe. He waves and Brendan waves back with that big grin on his face. There's a girl his own age, or a little older, sat at the feet of the guitarist. Her eyes are shut, as if in contemplation. She keeps uttering under her breath noises that sound like affirmation, encouragement. He sits against the fence and puts his beer in the shade while he watches her. Skinny she is, and dark, like the man. A boyish figure. He can't take his eyes off her. Then she rises like magic and walks over to where he is. She stands above him, a hand on her hip, and looks at him.

'Hello, cousin,' she says.

He stares at her.

'You're my cousin?'

'As far as I can tell,' she says.

She has a bottle of red wine in her hand and she holds it by the neck, relaxed and casual. She comes and sits beside him as if she's done it a hundred times before. He can feel her body heat against him. Her smell rises, like pond weed, sweet and heady. There's a grace about her, easy in her movements.

'Who is that, with the guitar?' he asks.

'That's my old papi,' she says. 'Your uncle.'

Frank is stunned.

'Uncle?'

'By marriage. On your mum's side.'

'Who's he married to?'

'Your aunt Jane. My mother.'

'Oh. We don't talk about Aunty Jane.'

He feels ashamed suddenly and feels the blush on his face.

'Why is that?' she asks.

'I dunno. A falling out. My dad doesn't speak about it.'

'Mum said something about that. She calls it racism.'

'Racism?'

'Where is he, this famous father of yours?'

'He's not welcome here. Gran won't have him in the house.'

'Never mind,' she says, 'I've found you now,' and she smiles at him.

He's bewildered.

'I knew I had a cousin, but . . .'

'But what?'

'I wish I knew before,' he says.

He watches the man lift his head to the white sky, scorched as it is, as it has been now for weeks, and howl to some invisible moon. Frank doesn't know whether to laugh at him or not. The call is pained, or so it seems to him. Raw, an appeal of some kind, to the core of suffering. Frank lets out a snigger. He isn't used to this kind of expression of emotion. He watches the man work the fretboard, watches his eyes and mouth and takes in the odd, discordant tones that resonate inside the body of the instrument. He looks at the girl. She's watching him watch her father. She chuckles.

'What?' he asks.

'You've been bit.'

'By what?'

'Duende.'

'What is that?

'You'll see.'

'What's up with him?'

'There's nothing up with him.'

'What's he wailing about?'

'About lost love.'

And then the man stops, as if it was nothing, and he puts down the guitar and takes a deep, intense drag on his cigarette. He looks across at Frank. 'Hombre,' he mutters, then turns, and begins talking to the gathered aficionados. The silence seems to creep back out of the hedges and flower beds, as if in relief. He looks at her. She's still watching him.

Frank holds out a hand, a gesture of futility he thinks, but she takes it anyway and holds his fingers. He can feel the burn right up his arm, a tingling. He holds on tight.

'What's your name?'

'Lucía.'

'Lucy?'

'No, Lucía,' she says, with a hiss, 'Loo-thia, like *thing*, like *thumb*. Th.'

'I'll just call you "Lucy".'

'You're a funny boy.'

'Am I?'

She touches his face and it's like no one has ever touched him before.

'Yes.'

She puts the bottle against her lips and drinks, then wipes her mouth with the back of her hand. He watches each gesture as if it's a revelation. He's under a spell. Her lips are wet and purple. She licks them.

'You want some?'

'I never drink that stuff,' he says.

'You never drink wine?'

He'd seen it in the club, behind the bar. On optics. One red and one white, but no one he knew had ever drunk the stuff. She takes his glass of beer and throws the contents into the bushes.

'Hey!'

'Shhh,' she implores him, and places a finger against her lips. She pours a few inches of the purple stuff into his pint glass and swishes it around. She sniffs it and takes a sip, then hands it to him.

'This is from my country,' she says.

He takes a sip and it rises through him, rich and pungent. Fruity but tobacco dry. A good hit. He holds the glass up to the light and scrutinises the brew. She laughs at him.

'What?'

'A connoisseur, I see.'

He takes a sniff. There are fumes in the glass, like you get with a whisky, but softer, fruitier. He knocks the rest back in one, and she laughs again.

'Olé,' she says, 'the wine of poets and of gypsies.'

She tops him up another few inches. As he goes to

neck it once more, she places her hand over the glass and stills him.

'Slow down, my little gitano,' she says. 'We have all night.'

'This won't last long,' he says, gesturing to the bottle.

'I have a whole crate of it in Papi's boot.'

He looks at her in wonder, and necks it anyway. He's beginning to feel the warm glow you get with afternoon drinking, the way it lifts you out of yourself, so you feel like you're floating.

People drink and dance as the garden fills and empties and fills again with music and song: punk at the top end, and the heady, demented flamenco nearer the river. The food comes and goes. People argue, vomit and leave in a stagger, while others arrive and stock up the beer table, the food table. Indelicate relations are struck up, neighbour to neighbour, marital rows drift in and out. There's kissing and groping and a few wrecked flower beds, much to the consternation of Gran, and all the time the thick, oppressive heat of midsummer inveigles itself into every cell. Eventually as the sun drops behind the woods, a less intense heat comes off the river as the shadows lengthen, and all the while Frank can't leave her side. She can drink the way his father drinks. She's beyond him. She holds some core of knowledge he has no inkling of. When his uncle plays, slowly, more melodiously, his songs of love and longing, it speaks to him of something ungraspable. When she talks to him his mouth dries up. He can only grunt in reply. She speaks quickly without hesitation, as if she's confident of every utterance.

She tells him stories about the past, before they were born. About how her father's village had burned and been destroyed by the fascists in the war. How they'd murdered all his family. Shot them all, against the wall of a cemetery. Shot all the gypsies in fact, children and women and many others too. Her father, his uncle, escaped aged fourteen by a miracle, and managed by luck and the intervention of God to slip through the eye of a needle into life rather than death. There was a ship that sailed in 1937, from Bilbao to Southampton, and somehow he managed to get on board. It was called the *Habana*. There were four thousand children on that boat.

He listens to her talk with a kind of awe.

He came to Scotland later, after the war, she says, and now here I am, and there you are. Which is another miracle. If he had not made it, then neither would I.

He lies back in the grass. He can't get it all in his head. He wants to ask her a question but he can't think how.

'I know,' she says, like she's reading his mind. 'It's difficult to comprehend, isn't it?'

Frank shakes his head and drinks.

'Well, we made it, Frank.'

'Somehow,' he says, but he's not sure what he means, and he watches her cross herself. He's never seen that before. He wants to ask her about it, but he can't begin.

'Where do you live?' he asks her.

'I'm in London at the moment, with my mum. At uni.'

'What do you study?'

'European literature.'

'What is that?'

'Books. Novels. Plays.'

He laughs.

'I don't have any books.'

'What do you do, Frank?'

If only she knew. Maybe she does. Maybe her mum has told her everything about the Bridges. How they're nothing but cheap crooks, how they murder people who get in their way. How they get pissed every night, and kick the shit out of each other. How their world is rank and full of ugliness.

'I work for my dad,' he says.

'Yes, I heard.'

'It's not what you think.'

'I don't think anything.'

She takes a book from her bag and flips through it. She sniffs the pages; at least that's what he thinks she does. And then she does it again.

'It's part of the ceremony,' she explains, 'when you open a book you smell its pages. It magics you away. Here, try.'

She wafts the pages in front of him like a croupier. He breathes in the scent. A vague smell of something. He isn't sure what: paper and her own sweet breath?

'What is it anyway?'

'It's Lorca,' she says.

'Who's that?'

'My poet.'

'Read one,' he says.

'It's in Spanish.'

'I'd like to hear.'

'OK. This is one of my favourites,' she says, and she flicks through the book to find it. 'Are you ready?'

'Yes.'

'Listen then. I will try and translate: No one fathomed the deep, magnolia scent of your belly, no one knew how you tortured the – erm, what is it? – hummingbird of love between your teeth. A thousand Persian ponies dozed in the moonlit plaza of your brow – and this line, I love it so much – four nights I clung to your waist, the enemy of snow.'

She stops a moment as if taking in the words. Then she looks at him and smiles.

'Your waist,' she says, and lays the flat of her hand against his stomach, 'the enemy of snow.'

'That's good,' he has to admit. 'And the hummingbird too,' he says, and takes her hand. 'Is there more?'

'Too much. It tears your heart.'

He hasn't heard anyone talk this way. He lies back against the warm fence. He can smell creosote and bracken. He sniffs the wine. *She's got me smelling it now*, he thinks. He sniffs again, deeply. The gruff sound of her voice fills him. It's deep for a girl, but melodious in Spanish. Sing-song.

'Read it.'

'OK. Hang on.' Again she pauses, to study the text, to think. 'OK,' she says. 'I search my chest – well, my heart, maybe – for the ivory letters that say: always. Always, always. Siempre. Siempre. Siempre. I love that. I can't do it justice in this brutish language of yours,' she laughs. 'Let me just say it like this' – and she brings her face close to his and whispers – 'the garden of my agony, your body, forever fugitive. The blood of your veins in my mouth, your mouth, dark for my death.'

Frank stares at her. He's never heard anything like it. She's turned and is looking out across the river. Her dark hair black as liquorice. It has veins of copper and wine running through it. If he touched it, he would probably burn. Then she sighs, sits up and pulls the cork out of the bottle. She puts the neck to her nose, then pours herself half a glass. She takes a drink and balances her glass on the grass.

'Do you smell everything?'

She puts her lips against his neck and kisses it.

'I can smell you,' she says.

His head is all over the place. He doesn't care.

'You know what that poem is called?' she asks him.

'What?'

'"Ghazal of Unexpected Love". It suddenly struck me, just now, how these things work.'

'How do you say love in Spanish?'

'Amor,' she says.

'Amor,' he repeats.

'And kiss?'

'Beso.'

'Beso,' he says.

She laughs at him and takes his hand again.

'It doesn't mean anything on its own. What do you want to say?'

'I dunno,' he says. 'Kiss me, or I want to kiss you, or I love you, or something.'

'I love you or something,' she says. 'That won't get you very far.'

'I can't believe we're cousins.'

'About 12 per cent of me is 12 per cent of you,' she says, and lays her head back in his lap and sucks on a cigarette.

'Which 12 per cent?'

'I don't know,' she says, 'the salt in our sweat. The heat in our blood. That taste in our mouths, when we kiss.'

'So I'm 12 per cent Spanish?'

'Well, less than that. If you can do the maths, of course. My mum, your aunt, is English, so maybe only 6 per cent.' She laughs and then she sits up, suddenly to look at him, with great seriousness. 'But all it takes is a single drop. It is powerful stuff, my little gypsy boy. You're infected now. By blood. Forever.'

He's drunk and dog-tired, but happy as a madman. The stars are out, and the garden is still. He pulls her to him and she lays her head on his chest, and he closes his eyes.

When he opens them, it's way past three and a moon shines. The garden is empty. Mist is on the river. It's warmer than any night should be. His shirt sticks to him. His head is spinning. He looks around the garden, a bomb site, just a single guy laid out, his head in the flower bed. He could have been decapitated for all Frank knows. It's close to dawn and a chalky light fills the woods and gardens. Stars are fading, winking out. He stands up, unsteadily. More pissed than he thought. She's gone.

Fuck it. He feels desolate. He wanders up the garden to the house. The doors and windows gape. The mass of the stone house sits. He can feel its weight, its gravity. He goes in the kitchen and sees his gran there, sitting at the table, as if she'd been there all her days. It's mercifully cool. She looks at him and smiles. She puts a Bible down on the oak table.

'What you doing up, Gran?'

'I can't sleep in this.'

He goes to sit beside her.

'What happened to Lucía?'

'She left hours ago.'

Frank bows his head.

'You're keen on her.'

'I've been bitten,' he says.

'She left you this.'

She holds out the book of Lorca she'd read from. He stares at it in a kind of wonder. He takes it from her and puts the book to his nose. He flicks the pages. He can smell her still, in the paper. He doesn't know which poem it is, that she'd read. It could be any. She's written a dedication in the front – 'I love you, or something' – and a phone number. His grandmother watches.

'We fix our eyes not on what is seen, but on what is unseen, since what is seen is temporary, but what is unseen is eternal,' she says.

Frank lifts his eyes to hers.

'That's like something she would have said.'

'Corinthians,' she says. 'There's poetry and wisdom in the good book too.'

'I know that, Gran. What's it mean?'

'What's already happened is passed. It's finished. But the future can be anything and everything.'

He tells her of the conversation he had with Laurence, about the finger pointing, the bad blood, that she must have been reading his mind, that he's heading off soon.

'Running away,' he says, shamefully.

'It's not running away, Frank. It's turning the other cheek. You don't have to face things down continually. It'll make you hard and unyielding. It's not a nice quality in a man. You're better off elsewhere. You've outgrown things here and your father is a bad influence. I think you know that, but you've always been in awe of the man, unlike Gordon.'

'I'm scared, Gran, to be honest.'

'Good. It's not a weakness. I wish your poor mum had been more scared. Maybe she'd have turned and run too. She'd still be here now if she had, bless her. That man is a monster. You need to find your own way now.'

Frank feels like weeping. He goes to her, and they hug in the gloom of the kitchen.

'I'm sorry, Gran.'

'I've got money, Frank, to help you on your way. It's no use to me, sitting in the bank.'

He wanders back down the long garden and sits on the riverbank. He takes off his shoes, his trousers and shirt. The Tyne gurgles, invitingly, sucks at the roots of trees along the bank. It looks purple as wine right now, thick and welcoming. A bat flits madly over the water. He wades in, it clings to his thighs. A silken texture. The riverbed is soft and muddy. He pushes out into the cool, baptismal water and lets it soothe him. He lies on his back and looks at the fading constellations. Something is shifting, and whether it's inside himself, or outside in the wider world, he can't quite tell.

sierra de cádiz 2003

It's pre-dawn. More silent it couldn't be. He's given up trying to sleep and stands now at the kitchen door. He looks out. The whole campo vibrates, as a cell or an atom vibrates. There is just the faintest intimation of a rising sun beyond the horizon, dawn flooding west, waking the people of Turkey now, and Greece, people rising for coffee, for breakfast. It sweeps onwards, lighting the hills of Tuscany, Sardinia. He takes the Redhawk from the dresser, the kind of gun that could kill an elephant. He checks the chamber and sits at the kitchen table. He cleans it with a tea towel. An old habit. Rubs until it gleams. What is he doing? He opens the cellar door and heads down the steps to where Gordon is sprawled, snoring on sacks. Frank kicks him awake and he sits up, startled. He rubs his eyes and looks up at Frank. At the gun.

Frank sits on a step and considers his brother. If you took them apart on the autopsy table you'd find the same bones, the same blood. Almost everything interchangeable. The corkscrews of DNA, the cells, the posture, the downcast glance. It's almost cool in the cellar. The light from the bare bulb lends them both a sickly hue. Things scuttle in the dark corners. A wooden floor beam cracks above them as it heats up.

'What are you going to do, Frank?'

Frank watches him. Broken. Pathetic. All the rage gone out of him. It should soften Frank's heart but it doesn't. He can't let it.

'You going to let me go now?'

'I'm not leaving you alone with Carol.'

'Please, Frank.'

'You put this gun against her head and pulled the fucking trigger.'

'It was empty, Frank.'

'That's not the point.'

'I was only messing.'

Frank is shivering now, from the chill, or from fear. He can't tell. They sit in silence for a while. The gun feels heavy in his hand. Hard and ugly. His hand is shaking.

'Did I mention they never found Lorca's body?'

'I don't know, Frank. I don't remember.'

'Well, they didn't.'

'Can we go now?'

'Not a hair off his head. They took good care to leave no trace of him. You need be careful if you're going to kill an innocent man.'

'Frank.'

'This place. It brings out the worst in people. You know about the civil war? The land was running in blood. There'll be bodies here, you know. In the olive groves. No one found their dead. Franco! Even Hitler hated him. This fucking country. The heat. It does things to you. It drives you crazy.'

'I don't know what you're talking about.'

'Don't worry. I'm talking to myself.'

'Remember the sticklebacks, Frank?'

'The what?'

'The sticklebacks, how we used to keep them in jam jars at Gran's house.'

The river light, how it played against the glass, the flash of silver fish in the water. He can see it clearly. His heart aches for it. He holds tighter the pistol grip.

'Come on, Gogs. Time to go.'

He gestures up the cellar steps with the gun.

'Where we going, Frank?'

He's worried that Gordon might jump him, so he stands back as far as he can, against the bottles and jars. What if he runs? Then what? Gun him down on the patio? He hasn't thought things through, but Gordon is surprisingly acquiescent, resigned. He stands and walks up the steps into daylight. When they step outside, the sun is already cutting deep shadows across the stone floor. The heat, even at this hour, is debilitating. Something stumbles in the campo, a goat or a dog. There's a clatter of dry stones, like castanets.

'I always looked up to you, Frank.'

'I'm your brother, Gordon.'

Frank's hand is shaking. The gun is heavy. He tries to keep it trained. They walk past the swimming pool, up through Carol's garden, past the lamplit pomegranates and onto the path up the hill.

wedding photos

The wind stalls briefly and the mist clears. Christ Church, Consett. County Durham in 1978. Days before flight. Before everything comes crashing down. This is the world they were born into. About to be shattered. The light and colour of a north Pennine town, the white, white dress. The family, if you want to call it that, the brothers in their suits. The symmetry. One of them laughing, the other one full of a dark foreboding, but which is which? It's hard to say, they look so alike. The Bridges at matrimony. The yellow roses. The white dress. A cold church, even in the warm sun. The light and colour. See the father, the grandmother, turned from one another. The conflict is palpable. Towards one side a blizzard falls: confetti, like a rainbow shot with a twelve bore. See how it shatters. It's in her hair and down her dress. She looks delicious. In one hand she holds the hand of Gordon. In the other, the hand of Frank, who is looking off to the hills, away from there. The ring on her finger is the brightest point in the universe. A beautiful diamond ring. Stolen from a jeweller's on Northumberland Street. Behind them you can see the angry skies, full of smoke, full of sparks. The steelworks of Consett.

The sky is orange. It blooms, thick and turbulent. The endless industry of coal and iron ore. But here's another. Look. Such a simple photograph, a snapshot that Frank took. Effulgent in the late light, elegant. She's in her white bridal dress. It's early evening by the look of it, by the way the light falls on the stonework, on the bushes. She's hand in hand with her bridegroom, walking off. She's looking back at the boy behind the camera. Smiling.

granada 2003

He drives to Granada. He wants to see the place where Lorca was killed. It's in the hills nearby. He parks in a shady side street and walks the empty road between Víznar and Alfacar. It winds through dirty scrub, a rough, demented land of stone and flint and the distant memory of water. A thousand stunted trees stand fossilised in the heat. Frank stands for a moment, taking it in. Beyond him, in the distance, he can see the vega, the fertile valley where the poet was born. It must have broken his heart to see it, in those final moments. He recalls Lorca's plaintive lyric for this place of his birth. *Down in the hollow lay the vega, swathed as it is in its blue shimmer. Through the recumbent air of the summer night floated the fluttering ribbons of the crickets.* It's almost in calling distance. He'll have thought about them then, as he stood waiting: his family, his precious sisters Concha and Isabel. It makes Frank well up. The irony is not lost on him. He won't go there. He wipes the sweat off his face. His white shirt dark and drenched. Flies buzz. Frank wonders whether on that terrible night the moon was out. That would be fitting for the lunar poet. He wishes he could come at night. To see it how he must have seen it, in his final moments. To smell the earth. How pungent it must have been, how heart-breaking: evening primrose, night jasmine. Which way would he have looked before they shot him? Maybe they'd have let him see the lights of his beloved Granada, the vast darkness of the vega to its west. Or maybe they made him turn his back. Such is the cruelty of man. Back then this was just a dirt road, connecting two filthy villages. Far from town. Out of sight. Cowards taking the poet in chains. The bullfighter too, and the teacher. Those great threats to civilisation, to put bullets in their heads. He wonders who they shot first. How terrifying for the last one. Was Lorca the last one? Frank stands out of the road, in the gravel, to let a motorcycle pass by. Two men. One of them spits at him as they approach. They know why he's here. There are Francoists even now. The pillion rider turns and watches him the whole way down the road. They'd kill him if they could.

He can taste dust in his mouth. It's in his eyes and hair, in the wet creases of his skin. It chafes like sandpaper. The heat is merciless. What now? he wonders. Everything has changed. His fingers are numb, his arm bones hum like pitchforks from the prang of the Redhawk. It throbs in the ball and socket of his shoulder, arthritic and dead. And yet nothing has changed. The world is just as it always was. Frank can't square it. He sits at the side of the road and lights up. What has always been simple now seems complicated beyond endurance. The way forwards the same as the way back. Past and future welded together in a monstrous amalgam. That look on Carol's face as he came down from the hill alone. She stood beside the pool as if she'd been waiting all her life. His heart was in his mouth. He felt desolate. He couldn't talk. She grasped him and they both wept. Maybe she'll go back home now, but he doubts it. He thinks of her in that beautiful garden, among her bees at last, her flowers and vegetables. Long, happy days in the high sierra. She can have Gordon's half. He watches a plane head south. It moves through the purest air. Inside his bag is the gun. He lifts it out carefully into sunlight and studies it. The elegant lines and curves, its blunt and pitiless utility. He stubs out his cigarette and takes a last look around him. A buzzard circles. Far away, sunlight glints in a kitchen window. A trunk road takes traffic from Granada down into Malaga. A donkey. The sky is pristine blue with a single white scratch.

acknowledgements

A big thank you to lots of people. Everyone at Jonathan Cape, especially Hannah Westland, Leeza Isaeva, Graeme Hall and Robin Robertson. Heartfelt gratitude to Georgia Garrett who had faith and brought this all to fruition. And to Helen Grant who kicked my ass and made me submit to the Deborah Rogers Awards, which is how this all started.

Thanks for all the help with early stages of the manuscript – it goes back a long way. Thanks Tom Vowler, Jacob Polley and Henry Shukman for their help with early versions. Big thanks to Luke Brown, who helped immensely with his close, brilliant and insightful editing towards the end.

To all at the Royal Literary Fund for hugely generous grants to keep my head above water. A stunning roll call. I couldn't have done it without you.